■ *The Secret of Blandford Hall* ■

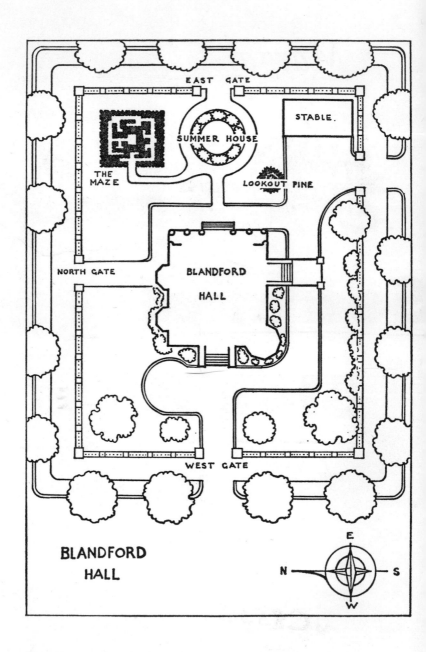

Margaret Crary

The
Secret of
Blandford
Hall

Funk & Wagnalls Company, Inc., New York

1

Dedicated to some very special
young friends of mine:
Michael, John, Steven, Lynne, and Danny

Contents

■ *The Secret of Blandford Hall* ■

1

A Stranger at the Gate

Bruce Blandford ran up the twisting stairway to the top of the tower. He raised one of the windows, put two fingers in his mouth, and whistled, two long and two short. Bruce's whistle was ear-splitting. On the lawn far below, Grandpa Blandford twitched on his chaise longue, and the morning paper slid from his face.

Bruce looked down at Grandpa fondly. From this height, he resembled a little old doll with a pointed white beard. In three years Grandpa would be a hundred years old. He had come over from England and had built Blandford Hall here in Iowa for his wife, Isabel, more than seventy years before.

Bruce leaned over the window sill, watching to see if his whistle brought results. It was a beautiful June morning and the whole summer vacation lay ahead. Bruce loved this view from the top of the tower. One looked down on everything from here, down on the tops of the Scotch pine trees, on the roof of the summer house, which couldn't be seen from the ground because it was surrounded by tall English lilacs. He looked down on the stone lions crouched on either side of the front door. To the south, the rooster weathervane creaked on top of the stable. Over by the north gate, he could see the twisting paths of the boxwood maze. The park sloped away from the house in all directions and it was a lush green from the June rains. Beyond the iron fence, the city traffic tore past on screaming wheels and squealing tires.

Bruce squinted down the side street to the south, trying to see between the rows of elm and box-elder that lined the street. A door banged and Moon Terpstra staggered to the curb lugging a full garbage can. He plunked it down, and after a furtive glance at the house behind him, loped up the street toward Blandford Hall.

Bruce let out another whistle and Moon answered. Down below, Old Fergus stepped away from the house, waved his arms at Bruce, then at the garbage cans, and at the same time he brandished a pair of hedge clippers. The message was so clear that Bruce

ducked inside. He'd do the work later. Right now he
had news for the gang.

Sticking his head up cautiously, he saw a flash of
red farther down the street. That would be Jean.
Jean, who always had a luminous look as if something wonderful were waiting around the next corner. In a moment she was joined by Honey; Bruce
knew Honey by the glint on the top of her golden
head.

The three came across the park and disappeared
into the house. Then Bruce heard their feet on the
back stairs. Now he heard them clattering across
the ballroom, through the billiard room, and into
the stair tower. Moon puffed like a walrus as he
climbed the steep stairs. When he reached the top
he flopped to the floor, moving his arms feebly. But he
revived at once when Honey uncovered four freshly
frosted cupcakes.

"Mom's painting," Honey said. This cryptic statement explained the offering of the cakes. When Lucy
Norton painted, Honey kept house, baked, cooked,
washed, and ironed. Lucy loved to paint big things.
A lion crouched on the landing of their stairs, life-
sized nymphs danced in the upstairs hall, and an Indian maiden endlessly paddled a canoe above the
sink.

"What's she painting now?" Moon asked.

"She's doing a ranch scene on the basement wall."

Jean eyed Bruce as she took a bite of cake. "Well?"

"What do you mean, well?"

"You didn't scream that battle cry from the ramparts for nothing."

"Well, I do have a little piece of news. Lord Hobart Blandford is about to pay us a visit."

Jean gulped at the cake in her mouth and said stickily, "But—but—isn't he the one—"

"Yes. He's Basil's son."

"But after all that happened, are you going to let him come?"

"Dad says that's all past history. Let sleeping dogs lie, whatever he means by that. Besides, they can't stop him. He wired from Chicago."

"What about Grandpa?" Honey asked.

"They aren't going to explain about Hobart. You know how Grandpa is, he doesn't remember anything for more than five minutes—unless it happened sixty years ago. He thinks Victoria is still Queen of England. As long as we don't mention the name Basil, we'll be all right."

"Does your father know anything about this Lord Hobart?" Moon asked.

"No. Nothing. You remember that Lord and Lady Blandford died soon after Grandpa came to America. He never saw his brother Basil again. He never wanted to—not after what happened."

"I should think not," said Jean. "Oh, how I hate that man! and that cold, greedy wife of his—Edith."

"I get chills every time we read about the quarrel," Honey said.

"Now that Hobart is coming, let's read that part

over again," Jean proposed. "It will seem so *real*. Where is the diary, Bruce?"

"In the billiard room. Why don't we go down there? You can read while Moon and I practice shots."

Bruce felt a little silly when they read the diary now. It was all right when they were little kids to pretend that they were living in the past and to think up those plays and games about knights and ladies and jousting tournaments. Now it was pretty corny. But the girls still liked it.

Jean took the leather-bound book from Bruce's hand and curled up on the seat beneath the bay window. "It's so exciting that Basil's son is coming," she said.

Bruce and Moon chalked up their cues and banked for the lead.

"He must be a creep," said Moon, "if he's the son of Basil and Edith."

"I wonder how old he is?" asked Honey.

"Dad figures that he and Hobart must be about the same age," Bruce told them, "and Dad is sixty-four."

"Come on, Jean," Honey urged. "Read the part about Grandpa's homecoming."

Jean opened the book to a well-thumbed page and began to read:

All during the long voyage, I looked forward to coming home, to telling my mother, Lady Anne, of my love for bonny Isabel McDonald and of my plans to make her my wife. I was eager to tell my father of life on Captain Moreton's Iowa Pup Farm, where sons of the English nobility were being trained to till the soil. I would tell him of the rich, black Iowa loam and of my dream to buy a thousand acres of the virgin land. I knew of Father's wealth in land holdings and of his interest in the Colombia emerald mine. Even though I was a younger son, I felt certain that I would receive a small share of the estate.

Moon snorted. "Little did he know Brother Basil, the rat."

"Quiet. Don't interrupt," said Jean. She continued reading:

That hope was lost the moment I stepped into Blandford Hall. My eldest brother, Basil, had come home with his cold wife, Edith. Somehow they had moved our parents into the north wing, and Basil had taken the management of the family affairs into his own hands. Basil made it clear at once that he meant to have everything, title and estate.

"Oh, the greedy pig," Honey said.

"Shush," Jean told her. "Now we come to the part about the portrait."

I shall never forget that night. I was going, with Mother and Father, to a ball at Lord Edmunds.

Edith and Basil would not consider attending such a dull affair and were preparing to leave on some gambling junket with their idle friends. Father and I were standing in the lower hall when Mother came along the upstairs gallery and stopped before the portrait that hung there. I must explain about that painting. It had been done on the Riviera when Mother and Father were on their honeymoon. Young Édouard Manet had seen Mother on the beach at Cannes. Struck by the beauty of her porcelain skin and auburn hair, he begged the privilege of painting her. Father bought the portrait, but when he took it home to England people were shocked. Manet had painted Mother lying on the beach with a sea shell held to her ear, and her feet bare. Basil hated it. He said it was common. But I grew to love the painting, for it was young and gay and the colors glowed with the warmth of the Mediterranean sun.

Mother was wearing her emeralds that night; the ear drops, the brooch, the bracelet, and the magnificent necklace—

Jean lowered the book, and Bruce saw the bright look shining on her face. "You know, this would make a wonderful play!"

Honey jumped up in her enthusiasm. "Oh, yes! And the *real* Manet is right there in the upstairs hall."

"The stairway, the stained glass window, everything is exactly as it was in Old Blandford Hall."

Jean twitched with excitement. "I can write it in dialogue and we'll act it out—"

Moon gave her a startled glance. "We?"

"All of us."

"Oh, no. Not me—not in a play. I'm all through with that stuff."

"Me too," said Bruce. He put down his cue, went to the doorway, and peered out. "Sounds like Cassie. But what in the world would bring her way up here?"

Cassie shuffled up the hall, her bunion-sore feet thrust into knit bedroom slippers. Her face was brown and wrinkled like a prune, and her thin white hair was twisted into a knob on the top of her head.

Cassie lowered herself into one of the shaky antique chairs that cluttered the third floor. She wheezed a while from the exertion of climbing the stairs. Finally she said, "Well, he'll be here tomorrow, and if you ask me, no good will come of it."

He, of course, could only mean Cousin Hobart.

"Mister and Missus driving to Omaha to meet him. Rubbish! If he must come, let him get here by himself. Me, I won't go a step out of my way to wait on any kin of Basil's."

"Cassie, do you remember all that trouble?" Bruce asked.

"Some I remember. Some I was told. I was born and raised in the big house. Mum was cook and my father was groom. When I was a young one I heard and saw plenty. Then, after Lord Cecil was gone, I saw his wealth wasted and gambled away. Lady

Anne's paintings sold, one by one, to pay the bookies and the sharkies. I saw enough, I tell you, to turn my stomach. When I was fifteen, Fergus and I married. We left Old Blandford Hall and came out here to William."

"Fifteen! Just the age we are now," Jean exclaimed, looking at Bruce.

"Folks used to marry younger, so don't go getting any funny ideas," Cassie warned.

"You'd better talk to those fourteen-year-olds," Jean teased, tossing a glance toward Honey and Moon.

"Don't exaggerate," said Honey, "a mere six month's seniority gives you no reason to be smug."

Jean did not reply. She had a faraway look in her eyes. "So tomorrow," she said, "there won't be anyone in the house except Cassie and Fergus and Grandpa."

Bruce knew something was brewing when she turned to him with a pleading look.

"Oh, Bruce, please, let's do the play. We'll never have another chance to use the stairway with no one around."

"Think how exciting it will be to do it *now*— when Hobart is coming," said Honey.

"Count me out," Moon said.

Jean held up her right hand. "I swear—this is the last play I will ask you to be in."

Moon groaned. "I thought we were through with those plays."

"You can be William," Jean told him. "All you'll

have to do is stand in the hall downstairs while Basil drops the painting on your head."

"Oh, great!" said Moon.

"And Bruce will be Basil," Jean decided, "because that's the most important part."

Bruce twisted his mouth into a sneer. "Out, you oaf! Back to the States! Egad, what a clod for a brother!"

"Save it for tomorrow," said Jean. "Now, I will be Edith. You can get your teeth into an obnoxious, hateful character like Edith."

"And I, naturally, will be Lady Anne," said Honey.

Cassie looked at Honey critically. "There's a ball gown in that old trunk in the storage room—it belonged to Isabel McDonald Blandford. If it fits you it will do fine for Lady Anne." She heaved herself out of the chair. "Bruce, Fergus says to tell you to set out the garbage and cut the lawn."

"Yeah, I know. I'll do it after awhile."

Cassie hobbled down the hall, and Honey said, "Cassie's really a good old scout."

"You know, it's funny," said Moon, "here's Bruce living in this big house with servants and all—most people think your folks are rolling in money."

"When we're really being chewed up with taxes. Who else around here has four acres of park to pay city taxes on? And two old people to keep for the rest of their lives? Dad says we've outlived our time. Probably have to give up Blandford Hall when Grandpa's gone."

"I hope I never see it torn down," Jean said.

"There's enough room here for a whole shopping center," said Moon, "and right in the middle of town."

"The land might bring a pile of money," said Bruce. "Then I would be sure of college. But what's the use? Only the guys with the scientific brains get anywhere these days. I don't know a satellite from a skyrocket."

Moon said, "I'm going to be a famous photographer and travel around the world."

"The first famous photographer to finance his career by selling nightcrawlers," Jean teased.

"I'm going to New York and get a glamorous job, like maybe modeling," Honey dreamed. "And I'm going to marry a rich, handsome, young, and successful businessman."

"That should be easy. They grow on every tree," said Jean. "I'm going to be a playwright and my name will be up in lights on Broadway. I can see it now—Jean Spencer's new drama—biggest hit of the year."

"In the meantime, you'd better get busy on that play we're going to do tomorrow," Honey advised.

"Thud. I'm out of the clouds," said Jean. "Let's go home."

Down below, Fergus was bellowing like a bull. "Bruce, you get that lawn cut before your dad gets home. You hear me?"

Bruce laid down his cue. "Old Fergie will keep yelling until I do it. I might as well get started."

"Meet me at Ned's after lunch," Moon said in parting.

Bruce wheeled the power mower out of the old stable that was now used as a garage and tool house. He poured the fuel into the tank and started the motor. As he put-putted up toward the house, his grandfather called to him from the chaise longue.

"Come here, Boy. Wheel me out of the sun."

Bruce set the brake on the mower, then moved the old man into the shade of the weeping willow tree. "There, m'Lord," he said lightly. "God save the Queen."

"Long live Victoria," wheezed Grandfather.

"Long live Elizabeth," Bruce corrected.

"Mind your history, Boy. Elizabeth lived four hundred years ago."

Bruce let it pass. Some days Grandpa didn't remember about the new Elizabeth. Bruce started up the mower again and made a mental picture of the square of park that had to be cut.

As his arms vibrated with the motor and his legs hurried to keep up, his mind galloped off on a jaunt of its own. *The motor hummed under the hood of his powerful sports car. He was the toast of the Ivy League campus, and the girl beside him looked up at him adoringly. With a mighty effort he ran the football over the line for the touchdown. He leaped into the air and dropped the ball through the hoop for the basket that would win the title. Now he bent his back to the oars. His racing shell shot across the finish line to the deafening roar of the crowd.*

He was jolted out of his trance when he hit the iron fence and scraped both shins on the mower. He pushed the stop lever and mopped his brow morosely. What was the use? There was nothing in life for him but grass-cutting, hedge-trimming, and garbage-carrying. A guy couldn't get a decent job until he was eighteen years old. There was no challenge, no excitement anywhere, anymore.

He was suddenly aware that he was not alone. An odd-looking stranger was leaning against the iron fence nearby. The man was barrel-chested and wore a striped silk sport shirt under a suit coat. The black felt hat he wore seemed strange for June. The opaque pallor of his right cheek was split by a thick red scar which drew up the corner of his mouth in a crooked grin.

Bruce had never seen anyone who looked quite like this man. He couldn't guess what his work was or where he had come from. Then he looked into the man's flat gray eyes, and a chill ran down his spine.

The stranger's eyes turned from Bruce's face, and in a long and insolent stare, took in the mass of pinkish stone that was Blandford Hall. Then he placed a cigar between his lips and moved off down the street.

2

Drama on the Stairs

Ned's Nook was down on the boulevard by the stop light. He sold comic books and paperbacks, and film and flash bulbs for the camera bugs. He swapped coins and stamps with the collectors. He sold used records—reject platters from the juke boxes. There was a pop cooler and a juke box and a little piece of dance floor in the center of the store.

You could get most anything at Ned's. You could talk about anything, too, because Ned was interested in everything that went on. And Bruce wanted to tell him about Cousin Hobart.

Ned looked up from his wheelchair and said, "Hi, Bruce."

Ned hadn't walked since the automobile accident that had injured his spine. A carload of students coming home for Christmas, an icy highway, and a newspaper headline—that was the story. Ned was young, still in his twenties, and it was tough to be tied to a wheelchair like an old man. But he never complained. He started a recreation league basketball team for spastics and cripples. They called themselves the Lame Ducks and played from their wheelchairs.

Bruce dropped a dime into the cooler and pulled out a bottle of soda. He straddled a folding chair and told Ned about Hobart's visit. Ned asked a lot of questions, and Bruce told him all about Blandford Hall and the story in Grandpa's diary of the family trouble.

"Don't let anything happen to that diary," said Ned. "Someone should write a history of your family, and the diary contains valuable source material."

"Maybe I will some day," Bruce said.

"You know, don't you, that the Iowa English colony vanished?" Ned asked. "Your grandfather was one of the very few who stayed in this country."

"Why did the colony fail?"

"Several reasons. The English were not used to the severe winters and were not trained for the rigors of pioneer life. These men were the younger sons of the nobility—*pups*, they were called. They were to be gentlemen landholders, and they planned to hire others to do their work. But the peasant immigrants from Europe weren't interested in finding new masters. They had come to America to take up their *own* land."

"So the English went back home and left all the good farms for the Swedes and the Germans and the Irish."

"Who have done very well for themselves," Ned added.

Moon came in then and headed for the candy case. In a minute his mouth was full of caramel and nougat.

"I have an order for three dozen nightcrawlers— day after tomorrow," Ned told him.

"Glug," said Moon.

"That mean yes?"

Moon chewed and gulped. "Sure, Ned, and thanks for the order."

"Business should be good from now on," Ned said. "They say the bullheads are biting."

The next afternoon Moon sat sulkily on the bottom step of the stairs and popped his Adam's apple up and down as he did when he was nervous. His only concession to the drama was a black bow tie. Bruce leaned against the upstairs banister looking very English in a cut-away coat, brocaded vest, and wing collar. Jean had stuck a mustache of crêpe hair to his upper lip. The sunlight, shining through the stained glass window, sent red and green lights dancing over his face, giving him a villainous look. As he looked at the window, Bruce thought for the hundredth time that the woman in the glass bore little resemblance to the Lady Anne of the Manet portrait. The glass was hard and cold compared to the luminous colors of the painting.

Bruce looked up as he heard steps on the third floor stairs. Lady Anne descended with regal swish and sweep. Her blond hair was upswept and the pouf of curls was encircled with emeralds. A ball gown of ivory brocade hugged her waist, then swept back in a bustle of tiny ruffles. Strands of emeralds hung from her neck and braceleted her wrists. Bruce found it hard to believe that this vision of loveliness was actually Honey Blake. And where in the world had she found all those green glass beads?

Jean wore an ugly orange dress with high collar and leg-o'-mutton sleeves. She had drawn vertical lines between her eyebrows and down the sides of her mouth. It wasn't hard to hate her—she was Edith, all right.

Cassie and Fergus came out of the butler's pantry lugging a pair of kitchen chairs. They sat down and folded their hands in their laps. They looked solemn and funny, as though they were waiting for church to begin.

Jean and Bruce retired to the end of the hall. Lady Anne made her entrance. She paused before the

Manet portrait, brought her hands to an imaginary clasp at the back of her neck, and began speaking:

LADY ANNE: Oh, there you are, William, and looking so handsome, too. I doubt there will be anyone at Lord Edmunds' quite so dashing. Darling, I may need help with this clasp—I can't seem to make it secure.

(*Edith and Basil enter along the hall.*)

EDITH: Mother! You're *not* wearing the emeralds!

BASIL: Didn't we agree, Mother, that you would not wear them again until Father got the insurance with Lloyd's of London?

LADY ANNE: But I'm wearing them tonight in honor of William. It isn't every day one's son comes home from America.

EDITH: (*crossly*) Those emeralds are priceless. It is ridiculous to keep them here. They should be in the bank vault.

LADY ANNE: And how could I wear them, then?

EDITH: It is hardly necessary to attend Lord Edmunds' stuffy country dance dripping with jewels. Don't you think that you are a trifle over-dressed for the occasion?

BASIL: I wish Father would *do* something about that insurance. In the meantime, it is most unwise to wear the emeralds.

WILLIAM: (*From the lower hall*) After all, Basil, they *are* Mother's emeralds—*still*.

BASIL: (*Leaning over the rail*) And what do you mean by that?

WILLIAM: Only that your concern for your future inheritance touches me deeply.

BASIL: Why you—you—*Pup*. How dare you come back from that God-forsaken place called Iowa, with manure on your feet like a common farmer, and talk back to me?

WILLIAM: It's high time someone spoke up.

LADY ANNE: William, please—

WILLIAM: Mother, I must speak my mind. Basil, for four hundred years our family has lived at Blandford Hall and loved it. *You* don't love it. You don't love anything but money. Your concern is not for Mother's emeralds—it's for *your* emeralds and what might happen to them before you get your hands on them.

BASIL: And *your* concern is that *you* are not the eldest son. If your memory of history is good you know that the eldest son always inherits the title and estate.

WILLIAM: Yes. And until now the eldest son has had responsibility and honor.

EDITH: *You* speak of honor. You, who propose to disgrace your class by marrying a common servant girl.

WILLIAM: Isabel McDonald is not common! She is as much a lady as my mother!

BASIL: You *dare* to say such a thing!

WILLIAM: Yes, I dare. It is as great a compliment to

> my mother as to Isabel, for they are the two finest
> women I have ever known.
>
> BASIL: If I have anything to do with it, none of the
> Blandford heritage will go to the offspring of
> a Scotch serving girl.
>
> EDITH: And don't ever bring her here to Blandford
> Hall.
>
> LADY ANNE: Edith! That is enough. I am still mistress
> here.
>
> BASIL: (*Shouts*) I'll give you a treasure for your little
> wench to stare at. Take this monstrosity! Take
> the Manet! I've always hated it, anyway.
> (*Basil lifts the portrait off the wall as Lady Anne
> leans over the newel post and screams.*)
>
> LADY ANNE: Basil. Don't drop it! Don't!

Grandpa walked in through the side door, tapping
his cane as he came. He stared at the scene before
him, then raised his eyes to the upper hall where
Bruce leaned over the banister holding the portrait.
Honey's necklace hung over the newel post. She
jerked back and the strands broke, showering green
beads down into the hall below. Then with a moan,
she collapsed and rolled slowly and gracefully down
the stairs.

Moon opened his mouth for William's next line,
but the real William Blandford took it away from
him. He shook his cane at Bruce and shouted, "I'll
kill you for this, Basil. If you have harmed my mother

I'll kill you! Come down here, I say! Come down here."

Grandpa's face was red and he breathed heavily. Bruce was scared. Grandpa might have a stroke! Bruce ran down the stairs, vaulting over Honey's limp body. Grandpa had a strange look in his eyes. He grabbed Bruce and whacked him painfully on the shoulder with his cane. Then, to Bruce's astonishment, Fergus started pounding him, too.

Jean had followed Bruce down the stairs. Old Cassie walked up to her, pulled back a hand, and slapped her face.

"So you don't think Isabel McDonald is good enough for the likes of you!"

"Cassie," Jean said, "it was only a play."

Bruce ducked away from his two attackers. "Yeah, Fergus—it's me, Bruce. For gosh sakes, I'm not really Basil."

Cassie and Fergus snapped back to the present, but Grandpa was still in the past.

"You cad! You caused Mother to fall. And her emeralds—her beautiful necklace—it's broken."

The old man dropped his cane and sank stiffly to his knees. He crept around on the carpet, picking up the glass beads. "It took us days to find all the emeralds," he mumbled, "days and days, and then we were never sure."

Bruce tugged at his arm. "Come on, Grandpa. Get up. We'll find them."

"Be sure you get them all, Boy."

"We will. We'll find every one. Come on. It's time for a nap."

Grandpa got to his feet and looked at Bruce. "Oh, it's you." He made no objection when Bruce took his arm and led him to the library.

Jean and Moon got down on their knees and started picking up green beads.

"Did you have to be so realistic?" Jean inquired of Honey who had come out of her swoon and was sitting on the landing. "It will take us half the day to find all these beads."

"When I act—I act," said Honey smugly. "For a minute there I really felt it."

"And so did Cassie." Jean rubbed her cheek ruefully.

Cassie shook her head. "I don't know what come over me. Seemed like I was in a trance, sort of. Sorry I slapped you, dearie. But for a minute there I thought you were really that mean Edith."

Bruce came back and announced that Grandpa was already asleep. "He seems to be all right now. I was really scared there for a minute."

Moon sat back on his heels. He complained, "I can't tell the beads from the spots on the carpet. Look how the sun comes through that stained glass window. It makes polka dots all over the floor and I keep trying to pick up the green ones. Say, Bruce, what are you—a drone or something? Why don't you help?"

"I'll get the vacuum," Fergus offered. "I think that contraption will pick them up." All appliances were contraptions to Fergus. He hobbled away to get it.

Cassie followed him mumbling, "Folks'll be back for dinner. 'Get out the best silver,' she says, 'put on the cut-work cloth and the candelabra, take the choice steaks out of the deep freeze,' she says, bowing and scraping to Basil's son—"

"Anyway," said Moon, "after this fiasco we won't have to have any more dumb plays."

"Don't try to kid us," said Jean. "You were having as much fun as anybody. You played William to the hilt."

Honey giggled. "Did you see Cassie's face when she slapped Jean? She was boiling mad!"

"You're not the *only* one who can act," Jean retorted. "Now let's go up and get out of these clothes. The boys can pick up the beads."

As Bruce pushed the vacuum cleaner he began to feel excited. Within a few hours Cousin Hobart would be here. Then, surely, they would have the answer to Hobart's unexpected and mysterious visit. The beads went clackety-clack as the vacuum sucked them up. When he heard no more clacking, Bruce unplugged the machine and wound up the cord.

Moon was stretched out on the floor with his legs propped up on the bottom step of the stairs. Bruce gave him a light kick and said, "I'll race you to the attic."

They charged up the carpeted stairs, clattered up the third floor flight, raced across the ballroom, and pounded on the billiard-room door.

"It's us. May we come in?"

Honey called, "OK."

The girls had changed to their own clothes. Honey was brushing her hair back into a pony tail.

Bruce peeled off the frock coat and ripped the mustache from his upper lip. He moved the lip up and down a few times, like a camel, to see if it still worked. He sneezed out the hairs that had gone up his nose. "No more of that stuff," he said firmly.

Moon shuddered. "We'd be dead ducks if any of the guys had seen us doing that play."

"Oh, you make me sick," said Honey. "What about Clark Gable? He was an actor and he was no sissy."

"He had it made," said Bruce. "We're just worms, fighting our way in a hostile world. We can't even get a driver's license until next year."

"*Worms!*" said Moon. "I almost forgot about that order for three dozen nightcrawlers. Can I dig in the patch down by the stable, Bruce?"

"Sure. And if you wait until later, I'll help. Then I can tell you about Cousin Hobart."

"May I come, too?" Jean asked.

"I won't touch the nasty things—but I'll hold the flashlight," Honey offered.

"OK. Make it about nine-thirty."

Honey stood up. "I have to go home and start dinner. Mother's still painting. Coming, Jean?"

Jean didn't answer. She was looking intently out of the window.

"Jean, let's go home."

"People don't very often open the gate and walk across the park, do they?" Jean asked. "And he is such a queer-looking man."

Bruce walked to the window and leaned over her shoulder. From this height, it looked as though a pair of legs were carrying a black hat across the lawn. Bruce recognized that hat. He had seen it only yesterday—on the man with the scarred face. Why was he hanging around Blandford Hall?

3

Digging for Nightcrawlers

When the others had gone, Bruce went down to the second floor and stood before the portrait of his great-grandmother. He wondered if Basil had lived long enough to realize that the painting he had flung so contemptuously at his brother William was now worth a great deal of money? Manet had since joined the immortals.

From what his mother had said, Bruce knew that the sale of the canvas could assure him of four years of college with plenty left over to save Blandford

Hall and buy all the purebred cattle his father and brothers could handle. It could buy a new house on the farm and a dairy barn with automatic milking machines.

The sunlight from the stained glass window fell on the face of Lady Anne, speckling the skin and lighting the smile that curved her lips. Bruce shook his head. It didn't seem right that any painting should be worth so much. It would be fine to have the money, but he knew that he would miss the portrait if it were gone.

Then he heard a car in the driveway, and he raced down the stairs and out through the side door. Their old sedan pulled up under the porte-cochère, and Bruce opened the door for his mother.

She smiled at him. "Thank you, Bruce. Did you have a nice day? Hobart, this is our youngest son, Bruce. Bruce, Lord Blandford."

The man took Bruce's outstretched hand.

"How'd yer do," he said, with a limp handshake.

Cousin Hobart was about Bruce's height, but stocky, and he wore a checked suit of rough wool— much too heavy for an Iowa summer. His puffy face was criss-crossed with wrinkles and was a startling contrast to the heavy thatch of neatly waved, ginger-colored hair. He smiled, showing a set of bluish false teeth.

Hobart looked up at the pink stone walls and shook his head in amazement. "By Jove, a miniature of Old Blandford Hall."

"My father brought the plans when he came back the—last time," said Gregory Blandford.

Hobart coughed. "Er—yes. A bit awkward, that affair. But ancient history—what?"

Bruce's mother looked uncomfortable. She said nervously, "Bruce, take Hobart's things up to Ernest's room. You two will share the guest bath."

Bruce picked up the traveling bags. His brother Ernest had been married for five years, but it was still Ernest's room to Mother. This meant that Bruce and Hobart would be across the hall from one another. This would give Bruce the opportunity to talk to Hobart about England.

Bruce put the bags in the room and hurried back downstairs to the kitchen. Fergus and Cassie scuttled in from the butler's pantry. It was evident that they had been peeking through the sliding window that furnished a view of the dining room and the side hall.

"He's got a shifty look," Cassie said. "I wouldn't trust him as far as I could throw a feather."

Fergus set some glasses on a tray and poured sherry into a cut-glass decanter. "Not as young as he pretends, either. My guess is he's older than Mr. Gregory."

"I've not a doubt there's something fishy there," said Cassie. "Bruce, fetch me some pickled peaches from the cellar."

"Hurry, Boy," Fergus ordered, "I want you to take this tray to the library. It sticks in my craw to wait on Basil's son."

"Do this. Do that," Bruce grumbled. Still, he didn't refuse. Fergus was so shaky he would have spilled wine all over the tray. And the errand would give Bruce an excuse to find out what was going on.

When Bruce entered the library he was relieved to see Grandpa sitting in his old leather chair by the window, reading the newspaper with his magnifying glass. He seemed none the worse for the excitement of the afternoon.

Hobart accepted a glass of sherry and held it up to the light. "I'm surprised to find you living in the city. Father always said William took up some sort of rural claim with the money our grandfather gave him."

"What? What?" wheezed Grandpa.

"Two hundred and fifty pounds, to be exact," said Bruce's father dryly. "At that time Iowa land was a dollar and a quarter an acre. Later, Father sold half of his thousand acres and bought this tract. Then in the boom of 1890 he sub-divided this land into town lots and made enough profit to build Blandford Hall."

"Always promised it to my wife, Isabel," said Grandpa unexpectedly. "A fine house for a fine lady. And I made the money to build it, in spite of that black-hearted Basil." He peered at Hobart. "Who is this fellow, Gregory? I've never seen him around here before."

"He's a guest of ours, Father. Wouldn't you like to go now and get freshened up for dinner?"

"Nope," Grandpa said. "I'll drink my sherry and read my paper. All the freshening up I need."

Gregory put down his glass and rose. "Would you like to see your room, Hobart? Bruce can take you up."

The three of them went out into the hall and Gregory turned to his cousin rather uncomfortably. "Hobart, I wonder if you would mind not mentioning Basil's name or your own relationship while you are here—for my father's sake? He lives in the past, you know. If you could make that concession to an old man we would all be much happier, I am sure."

"Ah, to be sure," said Hobart. "Let the dead past bury its dead, what?"

Hobart followed Bruce up the stairs but paused at the top to stare at the portrait of Lady Anne.

"I say! Grandmother as a sea nymph!"

"That's the Manet portrait. The one Basil—" Bruce paused in confusion, then finished lamely, "—gave to Grandfather."

Hobart laughed. "So you know that story. I suppose the old man talks?"

"Sometimes. But I learned a lot more about the family from reading his diary."

"There is a diary?"

"Oh, yes. Grandpa wrote all about his apprenticeship on Moreton's farm and his return to England. Here is your room, sir."

Bruce opened the door to Ernest's room and turned to leave.

"No, no. Don't go away. Let's talk a bit while I lay out my things," Hobart suggested. He opened a small traveling case and began setting bottles on the dresser top. Scents, shaving lotions, tubes and jars, and bottles of prescription pills and medicines. Bruce watched Hobart's hands as he fussed among the bottles. They were small, soft, manicured hands that looked as though they had never done a day's hard work. Basil must have had hands like that, too. He had certainly never worked.

"Tell me about yourself," said Hobart.

"Me? Nothing has ever happened to me. There's nothing to tell."

Hobart let it go at that. "This diary you spoke of should be a valuable addition to the family history. I would be most interested to read it."

Bruce backed to the door. "I'd better let you get ready. We always have dinner at seven."

Bruce closed the door to his own room and changed to a clean shirt. He felt very uneasy. It would be most embarrassing for Basil's son to read Grandpa's diary. And it was odd that he should ask to do so as soon as he had learned that such a diary existed. Bruce decided that he would ask a few questions himself. They knew absolutely nothing about Cousin Hobart. For all they knew, maybe this *wasn't* Cousin Hobart. Maybe this man was an impostor.

Fergus beat on the Chinese dinner gong, and Bruce went downstairs. He saw with relief that Grandpa would not be at the table tonight. He often ate a light supper in the kitchen and retired early. They could talk freely with Hobart tonight.

But Bruce soon found with dismay that his father had no intention of discussing family history with Cousin Hobart. They talked of politics, of high taxes, and of the trouble in the Near East. Then Hobart complimented his hosts on the tenderness of the Iowa steaks and the conversation turned to the raising of purebred cattle.

Finally there was a pause and Bruce asked, "What is your work in England?"

Hobart took his time about answering. It seemed almost as though he were thinking up a reply to the simple question. The three Blandfords looked at him as he took a drink of water, and then blotted his lips with his napkin. The silence lengthened. Then he said, "Ah—that is rather a complex question to answer. I have a number of—diversified interests, ah —which make it necessary for me to travel widely."

"And do you still live at Old Blandford Hall?"

"Oh, dear, no. The place has been a government building for years. My father, Lord Basil, lost it, you know."

"Do you have a family?" Mrs. Blandford asked.

"I never married. A rolling stone, you know."

When dinner was over, Bruce realized that they had learned nothing about Cousin Hobart. They still had no idea why he had come or how long he planned to stay.

Bruce changed back to jeans and a T-shirt, picked

up his flashlight, and hurried down the back stairs. By now it was dark outside and he flashed the light ahead of him as he walked to the patch of ground down by the stable. Fergus had told him that the nightcrawlers grew big and fat here because he fed them on coffee grounds. Bruce didn't know whether that was a scientific fact or one of Fergus' queer ideas, but Moon had worked up a thriving bait business and this was his best worm bed.

Moon arrived, lugging a syrup pail full of dirt, and the two girls came soon after.

"Nightcrawling" took concentration and speed, and left no time for conversation. Honey pointed the flashlight at the ground. The crawlers stuck their heads out of their holes and waved derisively. The hunters dived and snapped at them with forefinger and thumb. Nine times out of ten they missed, for the crawlers were faster than greased lightning. But once one was caught it was a great triumph to pull the long wriggling worm out of the ground. Honey watched and shuddered with morbid fascination, but the other three enjoyed their work. They each kept score on their catches, and Bruce finished with an eight-point lead.

Moon replaced the perforated lid on his pail and announced happily, "The price has just gone up to fifty cents a dozen. I'll make five bucks this week."

Jean scrubbed at her hands with her handkerchief. "We're dying to hear about Cousin Hobart."

"Let's go into the summer house," Bruce suggested.

The lilacs grew so thick and high around the summer house that the space by the door was barely wide enough to squeeze through. It was always musty inside. It was dim in the daytime and spooky at night, but it was private. No other member of the family ever went there.

They giggled as they fell over each other in the dark, staggering around, feeling for the split elm chairs. Bruce could have used the flashlight, but it was more fun this way. Honey squealed when a frog croaked and she refused to sit down until Moon upended her chair and shook it. Finally they were settled, and Jean said, "Well, what is he like?"

Bruce thought, what *was* Cousin Hobart like? He really didn't know. He told them what had been said, then how Hobart had asked to read Grandpa's diary.

"I know he's going to ask me to get it for him," Bruce said.

"I don't think he should read it," Jean said.

"But what can I say?"

"Tell him you can't find it," said Moon.

"But I can. I know exactly where it is."

"But you won't after I hide it. I'll go up in the attic and do it right after we leave here."

"Moon, sometimes you surprise me! How did you get that brain wave?"

"It's easy for someone with brains. Besides, if I hide that thing we *know* we'll never have to have another play."

"Oh, that reminds me," said Honey, "I told Mom about the play and about Lady Anne's portrait. She said she'd just love to see it sometime. Do you suppose she could see it, Bruce?"

Bruce wasn't listening, but he was sniffing like a hound. "I smell a cigar."

"Does Hobart smoke cigars?" Moon asked.

"No. He was smoking a pipe at dinner. And neither Dad nor Fergus smokes."

A stronger breeze rustled the lilacs and heavy cigar smoke drifted into the summer house.

"Let's have a look," said Bruce.

They tiptoed out of the summer house and parted the lilacs on the south side. The street light beyond the fence highlighted the trunks of the Scotch pines. They saw a spiral of smoke, then the outline of a man's hat. He leaned against the trunk of a tree—he had an excellent view of the house.

"Cousin Hobart?" Jean whispered.

"No," Bruce answered. "Hobart wore a straw hat —a very light one. Even from here you can tell that this one is black."

Honey whimpered, "I'm scared. I don't want to go home alone."

"Moon and I will take you girls home," Bruce told them, "and then we're coming back here and chase that guy away. He's beginning to make me mad!"

They left silently by the east gate. Bruce was sure they had not been seen, but when the boys returned the man was gone. They searched the park, but found no trace of him. Finally they went into the house where Bruce remained in his room while Moon made a trip to the attic.

4

Danger in the Stable

Bruce was always a little groggy when he awakened. The next morning he had forgotten all about Hobart when he went barging into the bathroom. He stopped short and stared in amazement at the face reflected in the mirror—a wrinkled face of pasty pallor with pouches under the eyes, the toothless mouth, a sunken hole, as the man shaved his face. His scalp was shiny and bare as a billiard ball, and a wig of ginger-colored hair hung on one corner of the medicine cabinet.

Hobart glared as he saw Bruce's reflection in the

mirror, and Bruce backed out of the room, muttering apologies. But twenty minutes later, when Hobart had emerged from his room, shaved, scented, and groomed, he crossed the hall and looked in on Bruce.

"Top of the morning, fella," he said jovially. "Shall we go down together?"

"Sure thing!" Bruce was sorry he had caused Hobart embarrassment and was glad that he had been forgiven. But at Hobart's next words his uneasiness returned.

"I'd like to have a go at that diary, old man. You could dig it up for me, couldn't you?"

"I'm sorry, Hobart. I haven't the slightest idea where it is," Bruce told him truthfully.

Hobart gave him a sharp look. "But you must know where it is kept."

"Things have a way of getting mislaid in a big house like this."

"But you could look for it?"

"I may get an idea." They were on the stairs now and Bruce quickly changed the subject. "I smell sausage. I'll make you a bet Cassie has scones and marmalade, too."

Grandpa was down for breakfast, and Hobart slipped into the chair beside him. "Fine house you have here. I understand you built it."

"Yup."

"Along in the eighties, was it?"

"Nope. Ninety."

"A lot of your things came from England, I suppose?"

"Some." Grandpa peered at Hobart. "You'd better stop talking and eat your sausages, young man. Cold sausage is indigestible."

Cassie slammed down a plate of scones and retreated to the kitchen. Bruce's father came in then and joined the others at the table. "Good morning, everybody. Beautiful day. I think we'll show Hobart the farm. You come along, Bruce, and drive the jeep."

"OK," Bruce mumbled through a mouthful of scones. Driving the jeep was a privilege he was allowed as long as he didn't go off the five-hundred-acre farm. His father thought it was good practice for the time when Bruce would take the test for his driver's license.

I'll give Hobart a ride he won't forget, Bruce promised himself. He choked with laughter as he formed a mental picture of Hobart bouncing on the seat beside him, his wig airborne over the fields.

Hobart foiled him, though. He produced a flat English cap with a strap that snapped under the chin and held the wig firmly to his head. And he seemed unconcerned with the jack-rabbit leaps of the old jeep over hill and valley. His only remark was, "Jolly good show—rather like riding a horse in the steeplechase, what?"

Bruce could see that Hobart was completely uninterested in the farm. He saw nothing fascinating about the new-born litter of pigs and nothing comical about the Black Angus calf staggering on wobbly legs. Hobart was only interested in getting back to Blandford Hall as quickly as he could.

It was late afternoon when they returned. As they drove past the Nook, Bruce saw Moon parking Ned's tiny electric car. He'd had it on the battery charger down at the garage. This was a service the boys performed for Ned. There were no doors on the car and it was operated entirely with the hands. Ned could pull himself from his wheelchair into the seat. He used the little machine for transportation from the shop to his home.

"Let me out, Dad," said Bruce. "I'll be home in a little while."

Ned looked up and smiled as the two boys entered the shop. "And how are things in old Piccadilly, by Jove?"

Bruce swung at him. "Just for that, I may not spend my dime."

"Anything new on Cousin Hobie today?" Moon asked.

"He doesn't like farms. And he's upset because I don't know where to find Grandpa's diary."

"Oh, he is, is he?" said Moon. Both boys laughed loudly and Ned looked puzzled. Moon bought a candy bar and began stuffing himself. Bruce went over to the shelf where there was a selection of new paperback books. He picked up a science-fiction yarn. *He blasted off and traveled by remote carrier beam. Then he checked his atomic disintegrator rifle, his cosmic ray vibrator, and the solenoid assentuator.* He was lost in outer space somewhere near Jupiter when he heard someone come in the door.

"May I help you?" Ned asked.

Bruce snapped out of his daydream and looked up. The man who had entered the shop was tailor-made, from his snap-brim hat to his polished shoes. He stuck out a manicured hand. The fourth finger bore a black onyx ring, centered with a flashy diamond.

"I'm Frank Olachnavitch," he said.

Ned shook hands with him.

Frank produced a legal-looking paper from the pocket of his coat. "I've bought out the Triangle Music Company, and I'm making the rounds to let the customers know about it."

Ned glanced through the paper while Frank walked over to the juke box.

"Nineteen-fifty model. An antique!"

"It works fine," said Ned defensively.

"How often do they change the records?"

"Once a month—when they collect their percentage."

"These platters are worn out." Frank dropped a coin in the machine. He shouted to make himself heard over the music. "This thing's a rattletrap. No tone!"

"The kids don't complain," Ned told him.

"Well, you'll be hearing from me," said Frank as he left the shop.

"I'm sure I will," Ned said as the man disappeared.

"What's wrong?" Bruce asked. "You look as though you'd bitten on a bad peanut."

"Know who that guy is?"

"He told you."

"Foxy Frank Olachnavitch. He started his career at fourteen by stealing a gun and holding up a store. Two terms in the training school for boys and one term in the state reformatory. He has beaten more raps than you can count. That's how he earned the name of Foxy Frank. Now he's gone legit and bought a music company. Ha!"

"What do you mean— Ha?" Moon asked.

"I mean, whatever he does will be good for Foxy Frank and bad for everyone else."

"What can he do to you?" Bruce asked.

"I don't know. But I'm afraid I'll find out before long."

"Ned, have you seen an odd-looking stranger?" Bruce asked. "He wears a black hat."

"No. Why?"

"He's been hanging around our place."

"What does he look like?"

"He has a scar on his face and he always wears the same black hat."

"Maybe it's just someone with time on his hands— perhaps a visitor in the neighborhood. You know, that house of yours is a pretty interesting place. It wouldn't be too unusual for a guy to rubberneck."

"At night, too?" Bruce asked doubtfully. He picked

up a candy bar and handed Ned a nickel. "Well, I'd better get on home. Coming, Moon?"

The two boys parted at the wide south gate to Blandford Hall. Bruce started up the driveway toward his house. As he passed the stable, the door opened and Hobart stumbled out. His face was chalk white and his eyes were filled with terror. His fat cheeks and mouth trembled with emotion. His breath came in choking gasps. He looked at Bruce without seeming to see him.

Bruce stepped up to him and took his arm. "What's wrong? Are you sick?"

Hobart focused his eyes on Bruce, then pushed his hand off and turned away without a word. Bruce watched him as he walked unsteadily toward the house, and disappeared inside. Either Hobart was sick, or he had had a bad fright.

Bruce opened the stable door and stepped inside. The car was parked in its usual place. He stood still and listened. There was no sound. He moved down the row of empty horse stalls and peered into each one. Piles of discarded furniture, lawn equipment, and tools were stored there. He moved a bag of rags and a mouse skittered away.

He looked up the stairs to the loft rooms where the coachman had lived in the old days. He started up. With each step he took, the stairs seemed to creak more loudly. He searched the first room and found nothing amiss.

The door to the second room was closed. It

shouldn't have been. His scalp prickled as he walked to the door and pushed it open. He stepped into the room. A pair of arms reached out and grabbed him around the neck, pressing powerful thumbs painfully against his windpipe.

Bruce saw the pasty white face under the black hat. The lips were drawn back from long teeth which curved inward like those of a mole, and the scar across the cheek drew a livid line from brow to mouth.

5

The Dark Tower

Bruce brought his arms up and clawed at the hands that held him but he was unable to loosen the vicious grip. He was being shaken violently.

"Snooper!" The man's voice was harsh. "You'll get what snoopers get if you stick your nose in what ain't your business. You'd better get lost and you'd better get blind if you know what's good for you!"

Bruce gasped frantically for air and gagged against the pressure on his throat.

"Now you get out of here and stay out," the man

snarled. He lifted Bruce off his feet and flung him against the wall.

Bruce gulped for air. *"Me* stay out?" he croaked. *"You're* the trespasser. This is our place, and you'd better quit hanging around here."

He pushed himself to his feet and backed to the door. Then he turned and ran.

His father was in the library, working at his desk. Bruce yelled, "Dad, there's a man down in the stable and he tried to choke me!"

Mr. Blandford looked skeptically at his son. "A man, Bruce? What man?"

"The man who has been hanging around here."

"Who is he?"

"I don't know! Dad, come *on!* He's down there now."

"Bruce, you're sure this isn't one of your wild games?"

"I told you—he tried to choke me! Please, Dad, hurry!"

His father sighed. "Well, we'll take a look." He laid his glasses on the desk. Then he removed his slippers and put on his shoes. Bruce fidgeted from one foot to the other. He thought his father would never get his shoes tied. Bruce picked up the poker from beside the fireplace. He hefted it. It would feel good to conk that mole fellow with this.

Bruce wanted to run but his father, who walked at his ordinary deliberate pace all the way to the stable, would not be hurried.

"He's in the far loft room," Bruce explained as they climbed the stairs. "I'll open the door, then we'd better stand outside and wait to see what happens. He's mean!"

Bruce turned the knob and pushed the door open. He held the poker like a bat, ready to swing. Nothing happened. They entered the room, but there was no one there and no sign that anyone had ever been there.

"He's hiding here somewhere," said Bruce desperately. "He has to be."

They searched the stable thoroughly and found nothing. Mr. Blandford dusted off his clothes and said impatiently, "Really, Bruce, don't you think you're too old to play cops and robbers? You have to grow up sometime, you know."

Bruce was deeply hurt. On top of everything else, his father thought he was a liar. Then he had an idea. "Hobart saw him, too," he said quickly. "That's how I happened to go into the stable—because Hobart came out looking so scared. We'll ask him."

Hobart was having a glass of sherry in the library. He was dressed for dinner and seemed perfectly composed.

"A man in the stable? Dear me, no, I didn't see any man."

"But—you looked so strange—as though something terrible had happened."

"Oh—well, there is this personal problem. I didn't care to worry your family with it. You see, I have a bit of a heart ailment. This afternoon I had trouble with my breathing for a bit. Nothing to get in a dither about. I was perfectly all right as soon as I took my medicine."

Bruce remembered the row of pill bottles on the dresser. Maybe Hobart was telling the truth—and maybe he was telling only part of the truth. Bruce was convinced that Hobart had seen the man who looked like a mole. There must be some reason why he wanted to conceal that fact.

Gregory looked worried. "It was probably that ride in the jeep that brought the attack on. If I had known about this, Hobart, I never would have suggested that you go. Shall I call a doctor?"

"No, no, old chap. I'm perfectly all right. My doctor gave me an ample supply of medicine for my stay here."

Then Fergus called them to dinner and the subject was dropped. Bruce ate in silence, and then went to his room, feeling disappointed and lonely. Whatever was wrong here, he'd get no help from his father. They'd just have to do it themselves. The gang had played too long at make-believe.

At least I can tell Jean about it, he thought. She had seen him, too. He went to the upstairs extension phone and picked up the receiver. His father was on the line, talking to Ernest about buying a load of cattle. Bruce gave it up, took a hot bath, and went to bed. His throat still ached but there were no visible bruises. If only he had something to prove he had seen the man!

During the night he was awakened by the sound of footsteps over his head. Someone was walking around in the attic.

Bruce got out of bed and looked across the hall. The door to Hobart's room was partly open. Bruce pushed the door open a little farther and saw that Hobart's bed was empty.

Bruce went back to his room and crawled into bed. After a long time there were footsteps on the back stairs, a shuffle on the hall carpet, then the creak of the bed across the hall.

Bruce overslept and didn't hear the breakfast bell, so that by the time he got downstairs the family had finished eating. Cassie gave him his breakfast in the kitchen.

"You look kind of peaked," she told him. "Feelin' all right?"

He nodded. Fergus sat down beside Bruce. He poured coffee into a saucer, then sipped it noisily. His palsied hands shook and the saucer knocked against his teeth. Bruce cringed, wishing he wouldn't do that.

"What was all that ruckus down at the stable yesterday?" Fergus asked.

Bruce eyed him warily. "There's a fellow been hanging around here—wears a black hat. You've seen him, haven't you?"

"No. I've seen no stranger. None save Hobart, and him I can do without. Now this forenoon you trim that boxwood. It's all higgledy-piggledy on the top."

Oh, what's the use, thought Bruce as he finished his eggs; there could be an army of thugs running around the park and my family would never believe it.

He went to the phone and called Jean. "Get Honey and Moon and come on over. There are some things we need to talk about."

"What's happened?"

"I'll tell you when you get here. We'll meet in the Maze."

Bruce went to the stable for his tools. He opened the door cautiously and picked up a heavy club before he advanced further. He searched the place but found no one. He picked up the stepladder and hedge clippers and walked to the Maze.

The boxwood maze had been Isabel McDonald's whim. She loved lawn parties and had pleaded with William to plant the Maze as an entertainment for their guests. Every year Bruce's father threatened to have it dug out, but Grandpa and Bruce wanted it left. So it had become Bruce's job to keep the leaves raked from the roots and the top squared off.

The Maze was simple to those who knew the key, but impossible to those who didn't. It worked like a combination lock, so many right turns, so many left turns, until the center was reached. Jean, Honey, and

Moon had learned the key long ago. Bruce was sure they could find their way through the Maze with their eyes shut on a dark night.

Bruce held the ladder against his chest and threaded his way to the center. Here two benches rested on a square of grass, a quiet hide-out where a person could neither be seen nor heard. He set up the ladder, climbed it, and snipped at the ragged shoots on the top of the eight-foot hedge. It would take most of the morning to square the top and shape the sides, for the thick growth went down to the ground. I wish I could trap the Mole in here, he thought. He'd have to dig his way out to escape!

He had nearly finished trimming around the square when he saw his friends coming across the park. He waved his hedge clippers at them, then climbed down and flopped on the grass. It was time to take a break anyhow—a guy couldn't work all the time. In a moment, the other three joined him.

He related everything that had happened the day before, beginning with Hobart's wig and ending with the footsteps in the attic.

"It's perfectly plain that Hobart is after something," said Jean.

"And the Mole is his accomplice," Moon added.

"If the Mole is an accomplice, why is Hobart so afraid of him?" Bruce asked.

"Yeah, that's right," Moon admitted.

"It must have something to do with Basil," said

Jean, "because the family relationship is Hobart's only connection with Blandford Hall. And he is awfully interested in that diary."

"Maybe he's going to steal the portrait," said Honey.

"He doesn't have to look for that," Jean pointed out. "It's hanging in plain sight."

"I know!" Honey blinked her eyes in excitement. "I'll bet there's a secret passage. Hobart knows about it because there's one exactly like it in Old Blandford Hall. Maybe there's hidden treasure in the passage and that's what Hobart is after."

"If Hobart knows about it, he wouldn't have to look for it," Bruce said. "Besides, there aren't any secret passages in our house. I asked Grandpa a long time ago. He built the house, so he would most certainly know."

"Well," said Honey sulkily, "there are always secret passages in the mystery stories I read. If there aren't any in your old house why don't you smart detectives think of something else?"

"Hobart must hope to learn something by reading the diary," Jean reasoned, "something that happened to William. We've all read that over and over. What could it be?"

"The way I figure it," Bruce said, "is that if Hobart didn't find what he was looking for last night, he'll probably try again. Moon, will you sleep in the tower with me tonight?"

Moon grinned. "You bet!"

"Oh, darn! You have all the fun," said Jean crossly. "There isn't a thing *we* can do."

"Yes, there is," Bruce told her. "You can stay away from here after dark. I wouldn't want the Mole to get his hands on either of you."

"Ugh," said Honey, "you needn't worry about me. I'll stay away all right."

Jean tossed her head. "I'll do as I please. I'm not afraid of you or the Mole or anyone else."

That was the trouble with Jean. She was as stubborn as a mule, and Bruce knew from long experience that it would be useless to argue with her. So he ignored her remark and said to Moon, "The folks are taking Hobart to the open air symphony tonight. It's a funny thing—it was Hobart's idea, and he doesn't seem to me to be the cultural type. Mother was delighted when he mentioned it, but Dad tried to talk them out of it. He hates concerts. Anyway, this will give us a chance to get all set. You come over about nine."

Jean jumped to her feet. "You big, brave detectives had better take your pistols and knives. You can use them on the mice up there in the attic! Come on, Honey. We aren't needed here. Let's go down to Ned's and see if he has any new records."

Bruce staggered up the twisting stairs with both sleeping bags draped over his head. Moon puffed behind him, carrying the lunch and shining the flashlight on the steps, for there was no electricity in the tower. Hobart certainly wouldn't go prowling until the middle of the night when the family was all asleep, but Bruce figured they might as well get set for the long wait.

They had fortified themselves with a thermos of milk, four ham sandwiches, a dozen cookies, and some bananas. Moon needed constant stoking to keep up his strength.

They arranged their sleeping bags on the floor, as close as they could get to the outside wall. Bruce had no desire to roll in his sleep and land on his head twenty feet below. This room was in the shape of an octagon, and had a seat all the way around under the windows. The stair entered the room at one side of the center hole, which was flimsily railed with widely spaced upright posts.

They laid out their lunch on the window seat between them. "I'm famished," said Moon. "Haven't had a meal for two hours."

In a few minutes the food was gone and they just sat, listening to the wail of the wind and watching the swaying tops of the trees below.

" 'Childe Roland to the dark tower came,' " said Bruce.

"What?"

"Something from a poem that just popped into my head. It looks different up here at night, doesn't it?"

"Yeah. I feel like I'm sitting in the top of a lighthouse watching the waves."

"Everything down there is full of motion—the

trees, the bushes, those towels on the clothes line—
everything seems *alive.*"

The boys stared at the scene below, squinting into
the darkness. Moon clutched Bruce's arm and pointed.
"Look."

A black shadow drifted across the lawn from the
stable, indistinct, yet free-moving. Then it disappeared into the shadow of the house.

"Cassie and Fergus have gone to bed," said Bruce,
"and they wouldn't hear a bomb if it went off."

"Then who—"

"Who do you think?" Bruce picked up the paper
sack and thermos bottle and hid them under a sleeping bag. "Look, if we're trapped up here we'll crawl
under the sleeping bags and lie still. Now, let's get
down on our stomachs where we can see if there's anything to see."

They stretched out on the floor and fixed their eyes
on the dark stairway. In a few moments, the doorway
below was outlined in pale light and they heard someone walking softly in stocking feet. Once or twice a
shadow fell across the doorway. They heard the opening of trunk lids, the closing of drawers. The search
went on and on. Bruce's leg cramped and he moved
to ease it. The boys began to think they were safe in
their hiding place.

Then a hand, clutching a billiard cue, appeared in
the doorway. A black hat and a foreshortened pair of
legs followed and the Mole began to climb the stairs
to the tower.

6

Foxy Frank Calls the Tune

The boys snaked back from the hole and wriggled to the sleeping bags. They flattened themselves under the window seat and pulled the bags over them.

They heard the Mole breathing more heavily as he climbed the stairs. Once he stopped; then his footsteps advanced again. Bruce lay rigid, wondering if the Mole carried a gun, wondering if, in case they were discovered, a quick tackle around the knees would bring down their adversary.

The footsteps came closer to the top of the stairs, then they stopped, and the heavy breathing seemed almost beside them. The point of the billiard cue poked into the sleeping bag. Bruce bit his lips to keep from crying out as he was prodded in the shoulder, the chest, the stomach. He tensed, expecting the bag to be pulled away. There were a few more pokes; then the footsteps began to descend the stairs. Soon the light was gone and there was no sound from the attic below.

The boys crawled from their hiding place and looked out of the window. A black shadow emerged from the house and moved across the park to the east gate.

"Oh, heck," said Bruce, "we could have tackled him."

"And get shot? I'm happy with things the way they are."

"You should be," Bruce said, as he rubbed his stomach. "Why couldn't he have poked you? You're better padded than I am."

"Next time *you* get behind. Then you won't be hurt."

"It will take some doing to get behind you!"

"Come on," said Moon, starting down the stairs. "I want to check something."

Moon went to the old wardrobe where clothing was stored and flashed the light on the garments hanging there. He fumbled in the pockets of Grandpa's frock coat—the one Bruce had worn in the play. "It's gone!" he said.

"What's gone?"

"The diary. This is where I hid it."

"Oh, fine!" said Bruce with disgust. "You couldn't have found a place more obvious than in Grandpa's own coat."

"Next time you can do your own hiding. What time is it?"

Bruce looked at his watch. "Ten o'clock. The folks will be home before long."

"No use sleeping on the floor now. Let's go down to your room and be comfortable."

"I suppose we might as well. We can keep an eye on Hobart's room and watch him if he gets to prowling."

They used the front stairs and Moon paused in the upstairs hall. "I'm hungry again," he said plaintively.

Bruce shook his head. "Man, where do you put it? Well, all right. Come on down to the kitchen."

As Moon started down the stairs something crunched under his foot. He reached down and scooped it into his hand. "Number five blue flash bulb. You using color film now, Bruce?"

"No. I can't afford it."

"Hobart?"

"I haven't seen him carry a camera. This is queer. Who would be taking pictures here in the hall?"

"Well, there's one guy who we know was here tonight. Are you going to tell your dad?"

"What good would it do? He wouldn't believe me."

Moon picked up the rest of the glass, and they went on down to the kitchen. Moon ate a piece of pie, and they were back in Bruce's room and in bed when the family returned.

"We'll lie here and listen to see if Hobie stays put," Bruce whispered.

Moon said, "Yeah," and in another minute he was snoring. Bruce was annoyed. As a detective, Moon was irresponsible. Well, he would have to keep a lonely vigil, as they said in the books. He rather liked the sound of it—a lonely vigil . . .

The next thing he knew the sun was shining, and Fergus was beating on the breakfast gong.

Two dozen pancakes later the boys strolled out through the side door.

"How about that?" Bruce asked, pointing to the weeping willow tree where Grandpa sat with the morning paper. Hobart had pulled up a chair beside the old man and was talking earnestly.

"He's pumping Grandpa," said Moon.

But Grandpa didn't seem to be paying any attention to Hobart. He went right on reading his paper. After a few minutes, he stretched out on the chaise, spread the newspaper over his face, and folded his hands over his stomach. Bruce chuckled. This was a signal that Grandpa wanted to be let alone and nothing Hobart could say would get a reply.

"Let's go down to Ned's," Bruce suggested.

"Good idea. He may have some more worm orders for me."

"Maybe we'd better take the girls along. Jean seemed sort of upset yesterday."

"Little pitchers have big ears," Moon observed. "Here they come now."

The girls wore broad grins, and anyone could see they were bursting with news.

"Well, good morning, Watson and Sherlock Holmes," said Jean gaily. "What happened last night?"

Bruce kicked Moon and replied, "Oh, nothing much."

Honey couldn't wait. "Well, it did to us!"

They told it in snatches.

"We took a little walk along about half past nine—"

"Around the park once or twice—"

"And we turned the corner and who should come right towards us—"

"But the Mole!"

"And he was smoking a long black cigar like the other night—"

"And he gave us a real mean look—"

"And he was wearing something lumpy on his chest under his coat."

"Color camera," said Bruce casually, "using blue flash bulbs, number five."

Jean's mouth fell open, then her face turned red, and she stepped hard on Bruce's foot. "Oh, you think you're so smart! And you make me so mad!"

The boys whooped and hollered with laughter. Jean pulled back her arm, and for a minute Bruce thought she would slap him. Then she gave up and said, "OK. Tell us what happened."

"Wait until we get to Ned's. We want his advice."

Ned was loading a revolver. "I just came from the sheriff's office," he told them. "I took out a permit to carry a gun."

"Why, Ned?"

"I've thought about it for quite a while. You know I carry the cash box back and forth from home to the store. My little electric job isn't exactly an armored car, and I'm not equipped to take out after anyone who should decide to grab my money bags."

"I wish we'd had you with us last night," said Bruce.

They told him the story and Ned looked grave. "This is serious. You can't have people prowling around in your house. You'd better get your father in on this."

"Dad won't believe there *is* anyone prowling around."

"There's something odd about the whole thing. Could Hobart be an impostor?"

"I thought of that—I even suggested it to Dad yesterday. He looked at me as if he thought I was balmy and said, 'That's impossible.' He said he's seen Hobart's passport and his membership card in a London club. He told me to stop imagining things."

"Why would the Mole take pictures in the house?" Jean asked.

"He could be getting the lay of the land for some

purpose," said Ned, "but if his motive was robbery, he certainly had the best opportunity in the world last night."

He wheeled over to the desk and laid the gun in the drawer. "You kids keep your eyes open and report anything new to me. I don't like the smell of this Mole character."

Honey dropped a coin in the juke box and she and Jean practiced a new dance step. Moon and Bruce shuffled through the pile of used records, looking for something new to them. They heard a car door slam, and the shop door opened and closed. Even with their backs turned they recognized the slippery voice of Frank Olachnavitch.

"Fine morning, Mr. Neeley. I always like to bring good news on a fine morning."

"Yes?" Ned's voice lacked enthusiasm.

"Good news for our customers. We've got exclusive distribution for a beautiful new line of boxes. Two hundred records—new ones added every two weeks. Our policy is to give our customers the best there is."

"What's the deal?" Ned asked.

"Same deal. Consignment."

"I mean, the deal on percentage."

"No percentage. Flat rate. Eighty a month."

"Eighty *dollars!*"

"Yeah! What's wrong with that?"

"Are you crazy? My box doesn't take in forty a month."

"If you want music, you can't be chintzy about it. Is it my fault you've got a hole-in-the-wall?"

"I'll keep the old one and pay my fifty percent."

"No, you won't. We're calling in the old ones— busting them up. They're obsolete."

"You can't do that," said Ned.

"Who says we can't? We own them."

"So the racket's come to town! And it smells to high heaven."

Frank looked ugly. "You keep your mouth shut, Small-Time."

Ned stared at him with contempt. "All right, you win. I'll do without music. Take your box and get out of here. And stay away from me, you slug!"

"Oh, no," said Foxy Frank, "we don't operate that way. You'll take the new box. And you'll lay the eighty on the line the first of every month. The boys'll be around to see that you do it."

He left and they heard his car roar down the street.

Moon let out his breath and said, "Gee!"

"Ned, you were wonderful," Jean breathed.

"Yeah, you sure told him off," said Bruce.

Ned's powerful hands still gripped the wheels of his chair and his face was twisted with rage. Then he relaxed and grinned at his four friends. "I suppose you kids would be happy if I'd take that fancy new juke box."

"Not from that thug!" Moon said.

"Besides, the old one works just fine and we like it," Honey said.

"Ned, what are you going to do now?" Bruce asked.

"I'm going to fight them. I'm going to fight them with everything I've got!"

"I don't understand this." Bruce was puzzled. "You own your shop. You can do as you please. Why don't you buy a juke box from someone else?"

"It isn't that simple. The Triangle Company has a monopoly here. No other company can operate."

"But they can't force you to take *their* box," said Moon. "This is a free country."

"That's what I think, Moon. It's a free country and a man should have freedom of choice in a thing like this. What's more, I don't care to contribute to the fortune of a mobster like Frank Olachnavitch."

"Why don't you call the police?" Jean asked.

"I plan to, but I may not get much help. From the bold way Frank is moving in, I figure he must have protection somewhere upstairs. There was a lot of outside money spent at the last election."

"Do you mean that we have some crooks at City Hall?" Bruce asked.

"I don't know. But, unfortunately, that sometimes happens."

"What can you do, Ned?" Honey asked.

"Well, first of all, I'm going to get on the telephone and call everyone I know who has a juke box. I'm going to try to organize a resistance."

"Oh, Ned, let us help you," Jean begged.

Ned looked at his four friends affectionately and shook his head. "You'd better not get mixed up in it.

These guys play rough, and I don't want you to get hurt. Now about your problem, Bruce. You keep your eyes open and tell me if this prowler shows up again."

This is what makes Ned different, Bruce thought. Most older people don't really listen to us—not really. But here is Ned with a serious problem of his own, and still he is trying to help me.

"I'd like to get a look at the fellow," said Ned.

"I wish we could get a picture of him," Moon said. "Then maybe the cops could identify him."

"Fat chance of getting a picture," said Bruce. "He's not apt to stand and pose for us."

"I have an idea," Honey said.

"Will wonders never cease! She has an idea!" said Moon.

"Be quiet," Honey told him. "Do you want to hear it or don't you?"

"If it's any good."

"Well, a couple of times Mom went down to the police department to draw what they call a *portrait parlé*. The witness describes the person they are looking for—maybe a hit-and-run driver or a burglar—and then the artist—"

"Honey, you're a genius," Bruce told her.

"What are we waiting for?" Jean asked. "Lead on, Norton!"

7

Portrait Parlé

Lucy Norton was sitting on top of a stepladder painting blue sky on the basement wall. There was paint on her face and on Mr. Norton's white shirt, which hung to her knees over paint-smeared jeans.

"Hi, pardners," she said. "Get off your horses and set awhile."

It seemed a good suggestion in view of the surroundings. A painted corral fence, draped with painted saddles, encircled the room. Behind it, painted horses grazed on painted grass. The painted sky stretched away to the purple hills on the horizon.

"Mom, we need some help," said Honey.

"What's your problem?"

"We saw a man with an unusual face. I said you could do a *portrait parlé*. They don't believe it—they don't think you can make it look like him."

"They don't, huh? We'll see about that." Mrs. Norton climbed down from the ladder and dropped her brush in a can of thinner. "I was getting bored with that sky, anyway. Come on upstairs and I'll get out my drawing board and pastels."

"Now," said Honey's mother, as they grouped themselves around her, "Take it feature by feature. Is his face long or round?"

Bruce closed his eyes and imagined himself back in the stable with the Mole's hands around his throat. The face had been close enough then! "It's sort of pointed, but the skin is saggy around the chin."

"Nose?"

"Sharp—and *up*—like this." Bruce pushed the end of his nose up with his forefinger, flaring the nostrils. "Then there's a scar from the corner of his left eye to his chin, and it puckers his mouth up on that side. And his teeth are real long and they slant in."

"What color are his eyes?"

"Like muddy water—and they stick out."

"Hair?"

"I don't know. You see, he always wears this black hat pulled down close to one eye so you can't see his hair, and not much of his ears, either."

Lucy's fingers moved quickly, filling in here, erasing there, and blending the crayon with little pointed sticks. Finally she sat back and said, "Now, how about this?"

Immediately, Bruce knew that there was something wrong with it. The features were there, but it seemed as though they were out of focus.

Lucy looked at Bruce's face and asked, "What's wrong?"

"He looks skinny."

"With those features he should be skinny."

"But he isn't. He's sort of *thick*. His cheekbones are high and his cheeks aren't caved in like that. His neck is muscular—you can hardly tell where his neck ends and his head begins."

Lucy went to work again. "My word, this *is* a character you've dug up. Are you *sure* he's real?"

"You bet," said Bruce.

The next time she showed the portrait it was the Mole—without a doubt. Honey shuddered and put her hands over her eyes.

"Where in the world did you see this fellow?" Lucy asked.

"We passed him on the street," Honey said truthfully. "I told you he had an interesting face."

Lucy sprayed the drawing with fixative. "Bruce, I'll trade you this for a look at the Manet portrait. I've never seen it, you know."

"Sure, Mrs. Norton. Come any time."

"I wonder if you realize the value of that portrait

—an original Manet! And one that has never been exhibited in a public gallery."

"I guess the folks know that it's valuable now. It wasn't when Grandpa first brought it over."

"Well, that's the way it is with fame." Lucy stared at the ugly face of the Mole. Then she handed the drawing to Bruce and said, "Now *you* have an original *Norton*. Who knows—maybe this drawing will be another Mona Lisa."

"You're late for lunch," Cassie informed Bruce as he came in through the kitchen door. He ran up the back stairs, hid the drawing of the Mole in the bottom drawer of his dresser, then hurried down to the dining room and slid into his chair under the disapproving eye of his mother. The others had nearly finished eating. Hobart announced that he had some affairs to see about and would take a bus downtown. He excused himself, and a moment later Bruce saw him leave the house and walk across the park, his straw hat perched jauntily on the side of the ginger wig.

Bruce went back to his room and opened the drawer, planning to get a better look at the drawing. Then he heard his mother coming down the hall. She looked in from the doorway.

"Oh, Bruce, *do* close your dresser drawers. They look so messy standing open. And please gather up those soiled clothes and throw them in the hamper."

Bruce willingly slammed the drawer shut—he didn't want to try to explain that drawing to his mother. Then he hustled around picking up his clothes.

His mother stood in the door with a puzzled look on her face. "Now, why did I come down here?" she asked.

"I don't know," said Bruce.

"Oh, yes, I thought I'd better check Hobart's room while he's away. Cassie absolutely refuses to do a thing for him. All she does is babble about Basil. Good heavens, that trouble happened when she was a little girl. Most of what she remembers is probably servants' gossip."

She opened the door across the hall and Bruce followed her into the room. It was quite neat, and Mrs. Blandford sighed with relief.

"Well, Hobart does pick up after himself. I'll just give it a lick and a promise." She flicked a duster over the dresser top. "Goodness, what a lot of medicine bottles. I wonder if his heart really is bad. You know, Bruce, it seems strange to me that Hobart says nothing about how long he plans to stay. I do think house guests should announce their plans. It's such a worry not to know what to expect."

"I think it's queer we don't know *why* he came," Bruce said. "People don't just drop in from England."

"No, they don't. And to tell you the truth, I feel a little uneasy about Hobart. But you know how your father is. He accepts everyone at face value."

Everyone except me, Bruce thought bitterly. We operate on different wave lengths.

His mother removed a coat from the back of a chair, put it on a hanger, and hung it in the closet. Bruce noticed that the pocket sagged heavily.

"There, I think that will do for now," said Mrs. Blandford. "Oh, yes, Fergus expects you to finish the mowing. He said you were 'gallivantin'' all morning."

"All right, I will. Mother, Mrs. Norton wants to see the Manet."

"Lucy Norton? Oh, yes, she paints, doesn't she? Why, of course, I'd love to have her see it. Let's see, tomorrow I have a luncheon date. Your father and Ernest are cutting the first alfalfa and you are to help. You tell her to come on Friday, and we'll have a cup of tea."

Mrs. Blandford went back down the hall. Bruce waited until she was out of sight; then, feeling very guilty, he slipped into Hobart's room and reached into the coat pocket. His guess had been correct. He pulled out Grandpa's diary and along with it a folded news sheet. The heading on it read RACING FORM. He couldn't make head nor tail of it, but he knew it concerned horse racing. He put the things back in the coat and hung the coat over the back of the chair where his mother had found it.

His discovery confirmed his conviction that Hobart *had* seen the Mole, not only once, but a second time, when he must have obtained the diary. It was clear that Hobart wanted to conceal these meetings, and that there was some connection between these two that promised no good for those at Blandford Hall.

Bruce went to the stable to get the lawn mower. Ever since his encounter there with the Mole he entered cautiously. He looked around downstairs, then decided to check above. The far room was not as it had been. Someone had carried up two chairs from below and the stale smell of cigar smoke hung in the air. Was Hobart meeting the Mole here every night? What did they talk about? Bruce felt that he must find the answer to this puzzle—there was no one else to do it.

Bruce made himself a little cave in the old horse stall near the stairs. He moved the cast-off furniture out from the wall, then tossed an old quilt over the furniture. This concealed his hideaway from others but left him a clear view of the stairs.

Then he took out the mower and worked quickly and steadily. He would finish the lawn, then sleep until dinner time. A long nap would help him to stay awake later on.

It seemed to Bruce that hours had passed since he had crawled into his hole. The gray twilight turned to pitch dark. There was no sound in the stable except the occasional skittering of field mice. Down on the boulevard, car horns tooted and tires squealed.

The longer Bruce sat hunched in his hole, the smaller and more cramped the space seemed. He was bored and began to feel foolish. A fine way to spend the night, huddled under a bunch of broken-down chairs! The Mole was probably gone—maybe for good. He felt in his pocket for the back-door key. He wondered if Fergus would raise a fuss when he found it gone. He hoped that his mother wouldn't come to his room tonight. He had put his football helmet and his shoulder pads under the blanket.

The chimes on Saint Pat's struck ten—ten-thirty—then eleven. In spite of his nap, he was beginning to feel sleepy—sitting so long without moving and with nothing to do.

Then he heard the footsteps. The door made only a whisper as it opened. Then a pencil-thin line of light on the stairs, the sound of footsteps ascending, the squeak of a chair overhead, and the odor of cigar smoke drifting down.

Bruce felt that it must have been ten or fifteen minutes later when the door opened again and more steps ascended, slower steps this time. Then the murmur of voices. Bruce wriggled closer to the stairway and strained to hear, but he could not distinguish the words.

Then a voice was raised in anger. "I've had enough of your cock-and-bull stories! You had better deliver —and soon!"

Bruce could not hear the reply, but the first voice grated, "Time? There isn't any time. And another thing, you'd better figure out a way to keep those kids from snooping or they're gonna get hurt."

The voices dropped again and the murmuring went on for some time. Then Bruce caught the fragment, "—don't like it. Those things are hot to handle. But we'll try it."

Chairs scraped and footsteps approached the stairs. For the first time, Bruce heard Hobart's voice clearly, "Tomorrow night at eleven."

After Hobart left, the Mole made no move to depart. Bruce wondered if he would have to spend the night in his hole. Maybe if he crept on hands and knees he could get out silently. No, he decided, it was too risky. He must cross the open park to get to the house and the Mole was probably watching from the upstairs window. He thought about tomorrow night. He must get himself a place where he could hear. He *must* find out what Hobart was up to.

A chair was moved overhead and footsteps approached the top of the stairs, then stopped. The bright circle from a flashlight showed on the steps. Then the stable door pushed open, the light lifted, but Bruce could not see the face it illumined.

Then the Mole said, "OK, Frankie. Come on up."

8

The Racket Moves In

Bruce's heart pounded with excitement. If this was Frankie Olachnavitch, it meant that his problem and Ned's problem were somehow connected. If he only could *hear*. He wriggled closer to the stairway, and laid his ear to the floor, but it was useless. They kept their voices low. The conversation went on for a long time. Then chairs scraped, and Bruce scarcely had time to back into his hole before the two men began to descend the stairs.

"I gotta keep the finger on this English bloke," the

Mole said. "You must handle the other end. Now tomorrow you start delivery."

"Right, Gito."

"Leave the hold-out until last. He may fall into line. Get the job done in one day, and make 'em think they're getting something choice. Don't give 'em time to talk it over—"

The door opened and closed. In a moment Bruce heard a car start up and drive away. He crawled out of his hiding place and stretched his arms and legs. Then he opened the door and looked around. Nothing moved in the park. Blandford Hall was dark except for one window. There was a light behind the drawn shade of Hobart's room.

Bruce crossed the park and opened the kitchen door quietly. He took off his shoes and crept up the back stairs. Hobart's door was tightly closed. Bruce glanced down the hall to the front of the house. At once he realized that something was wrong. This wall was customarily hung with half a dozen oil paintings in heavy frames. Now the only painting hanging there was the Manet!

Bruce went into his room and undressed. His head whirled. It didn't make sense. The Manet was the only valuable painting they owned. What had happened to the others? And why was that one left? At least, Bruce reasoned, the folks can't very well ignore five missing paintings. Now they will have to believe that there is something going on.

The barest whisper of sound came from the hall—

the shush of feet on carpet, moving back and forth. Hobart was on the prowl again—this time in the upstairs hall. For a heavy man, he was very quiet. In a few moments came a new sound—water running in the bathroom.

Bruce got out of bed and stepped into the hall. Hobart came out of the bathroom. He was carrying a glass of water and his hand shook so that the water slopped over onto the carpet. His face was gray, his mouth jerked nervously, and his bald head was beaded with drops of perspiration.

"Hobart, are you sick?" Bruce whispered.

Hobart gave him a venomous look. "Let me alone, you hear? Just let me alone and mind your own business!"

Hobart went into his bedroom and closed the door. Bruce looked down the hall. All the portraits were now hanging in their usual places! Bruce tiptoed to the nearest painting and put his hand behind it. The brittle, old, paper backing had been glued to the frames. Now his fingers touched smooth, strong paper and fresh masking tape.

He didn't find what he is looking for, Bruce guessed, and he is getting more frightened all the time.

He went back to bed, puzzling over the conversation in the stable. He had heard Frankie speak only two words, but he thought the man must be Olachnavitch, and the delivery must mean the new juke boxes.

Bruce's first thought in the morning was to get down to the Nook and tell Ned what he had heard. But he had forgotten about the haying. His father was almost through eating when Bruce arrived at the table.

"Hurry up, son. I told Ernest we would be at the farm by eight."

I'll telephone, thought Bruce, as he gulped his orange juice and started on his eggs. But before he had finished, his father was honking the horn under the porte-cochère, and Bruce didn't dare to keep him waiting. Hobart hadn't come down. Bruce left Cassie grumbling that *she* certainly wouldn't fix him a special meal if he couldn't get up mornings like other folks.

Usually Bruce enjoyed running the farm machinery, but today he was impatient to finish and get back to town. He worked too fast, and had to go back over several swaths that he had missed. At noon he suggested that they leave the last field and do it another day, but his brother vetoed the idea.

"It's right to cut now," said Ernest. "On a farm, you do things when the time is right. What ails you today, Bruce? Is your girl waiting for you?"

So they had finished the job, and even then Mr. Blandford stood leaning against the barn, talking to Ernest and the hired man. It was four o'clock when they left the farm and then, when they came into town, they hit the five-o'clock traffic and had to crawl along. Bruce felt that he had lived a lifetime when

he finally jumped out of the car and opened the gate
to the park. His father drove on to the stable and
Bruce raced for the house.

He entered the side door and started up the stairs.
The sunlight streamed through the stained glass window and dappled the bare wall where the Manet portrait should hang. His eyes traveled along the wall.
All the other portraits were in place—but the Manet
was gone!

Bruce remembered that it was Thursday. Cassie
and Fergus would have been out all afternoon. His
mother had gone to a bridge luncheon. Except for
Grandpa, Hobart had been alone in the house.

Bruce ran to the stable where his father was re-
moving farm produce from the car trunk.

"Dad! The Manet portrait is gone!"

Mr. Blandford turned and gave him a skeptical
look. "Now, Bruce, that's impossible."

"Dad, I couldn't be mistaken about a thing like
that!"

"All right, we'll see. Here, help me carry this stuff
up to the kitchen."

With maddening deliberation, he handed Bruce
a basket of eggs and two dressed chickens. I *would*
get the eggs, Bruce fumed to himself. How can you
hurry with a basket of eggs? His father picked up the
paper bags filled with garden greens, and they started
for the house at a slow walk. They deposited the food
in the kitchen. When they reached the front hall and
looked up, the Manet portrait hung in its usual place!

Gregory Blandford shook his head. "Bruce, what's wrong with you? This sort of thing isn't funny, you know."

"But it *was* gone! Dad, you must believe me!"

"I believe what I see. And there it is."

There it was indeed. Bruce felt hopeless and scared. Tears smarted behind his eyes as he ran up the stairs and down the hall to his room. He could hear Hobart moving around across the hall. It was clear what had happened. Hobart had been examining the Manet when Bruce arrived. He had replaced it while Bruce was bringing his father to the house.

Bruce washed up and changed his clothes. Then he called Jean from the upstairs extension phone. "Can you find Moon and Honey? We have to get down to Ned's."

"Now?"

"Yes, now."

"What's happened?"

"I'll tell you later. Hurry, will you?"

Bruce banged the back door and loped across the park. Fergus, on his way from the bus stop, called out, "Whoa, boy." But Bruce kept on going.

Down the street he waited for Moon, who trotted up, puffing and complaining. "Hey, Bruce, what's—the—all—fired—rush?"

"Save your wind, Moon," Bruce advised him. Then he cupped his hands, and yelled at the two girls who were a block behind. "Run, run, *run!*"

When the four of them turned the corner into the

avenue, they saw a truck parked outside the door of Ned's Nook. On the sidewalk was a juke box, sparkling with colored glass and nickel-plated buttons. Then they heard several sharp explosions, much like the backfiring of a car. Two men ran out of the shop. They picked up the juke box, heaved it into the truck, and roared off down the street.

Bruce was the first one through the door. Ned lay on the floor. The wheelchair was overturned beside him. His eyes were closed, and blood trickled from the corner of his mouth.

9

Cats in the Pine Tree

Bruce dropped to his knees beside Ned. "I think he's dead."

"Oh, no," Jean cried. "He can't be. Not Ned."

"Those rats," Moon said. "They shot him. That's what we heard."

Ned opened one eye and winked. At the same time, he waved the gun in his right hand. "It was my gun you heard. It takes more than two thugs to get one old cripple."

Bruce breathed a sigh of relief, and Moon jumped to right the wheelchair. Honey knelt down and wiped the blood off Ned's mouth with her handkerchief. "But you *are* hurt," she said.

Ned moved his jaw gingerly. "Knocked around some," he admitted. "Now get me up there and I'll take stock."

They lifted him into his wheelchair, and he trundled over to the lavatory with the mirror above it. He tested his teeth between thumb and forefinger. "None of 'em seems to be loose."

"Don't you want me to call the police?" Bruce asked.

"Now don't rush me," said Ned, dashing cold water over his face. He stared at himself in the mirror. "You know, I think I'm going to get a dandy shiner out of this."

The four friends stared at him in amazement.

"You sound happy about it," Jean said.

"I am. When you've been removed from combat as long as I have, a good fight really sets you up. I won, you know!"

"You won?"

"Sure. I told them I wouldn't take their juke box —and I didn't."

Jean looked around. "The old one's gone."

"Yep."

"Tell us what happened, Ned."

"Well, a truck barreled up a while ago with the new box in it. These two men came in and said they were making a delivery for the Triangle Music Company. I pointed to the old box and said, 'All right, you can take that out.' I didn't want anything around here that belonged to Foxy Frank. They carried it out and loaded it. Then they took the new box out of the truck. I said, 'You can put that back. I'm not taking it.'

" 'Oh, yes, you are,' said this one muscle man.

"I put my wheelchair in the doorway and sat there blocking the entrance. They stood there a minute, looking mean. Then Muscles came up and kicked the chair and shoved me back into the shop. They both came at me and started using me for a punching bag. But I landed a few myself, and that made them mad. They tipped my chair over and Muscles got ready to kick me. I pulled the gun out of my jacket pocket and shot between his legs. I gave them two or three more—close enough to scare them, and they skedaddled out of here."

"Golly!" said Honey.

Jean's eyes glistened as she said, "I think that's the bravest thing I ever heard of!"

Bruce felt the same way, but of course he couldn't say so. That would be embarrassing. But he did have a sudden understanding of Ned's feelings. There must be a kind of glory in fighting for something you really believed in! He stood there, imagining how it would be, savoring the thrill of it. Then he remembered why he had come.

"Ned," he said. "Foxy Frank and the Mole are in this together."

"How do you know that?"

Bruce recounted the story of the night before.

"Good work!" Ned said warmly. "Now we know for certain that the Mole has some hold over your cousin, and that Hobart is probably his unwilling accomplice. We know that Frank is working with the Mole, and they are meeting in your stable. It's pretty evident that organized crime is moving into the juke box business in our town."

"Can't the police take it from here?" Jean asked.

"Now let's think what real evidence we have," Ned counseled. "First, no one has actually seen the Mole except you four. We have the scraps of conversation Bruce overheard in the stable, but only Bruce's word for that. Only Bruce saw the portrait switching. There are no witnesses to the attack on me. You four found me, but I could have fallen over and injured myself, and made up the story to frame Foxy Frank."

"You wouldn't do that," said Honey.

"No, I wouldn't. But I could have."

"The way you tell it," Jean said, "it sounds as though we don't have *any* evidence."

"We don't, really. Not sound evidence that would stand up in court."

"Another thing," said Bruce thoughtfully, "if we call in the police now, the Mole may fade away, and we will never know who he really is or what he's after. I *know* they're going to meet again tonight. I wish we could figure out some way to hear everything that's said."

"There might be a way," Ned told him. "I have a friend who sells all kinds of recording gadgets.

There is a machine called a detectaphone. It's often used by the police. You plant a little microphone in a concealed spot. A wire runs from the mike to another room where the recorder is placed."

Bruce was enthusiastic. "There are plenty of little holes in that upstairs room, and the recorder could go into one of the stalls below. We can find out what Hobart is after, and get the goods on Foxy Frank and the Mole at the same time!"

"There's one thing," Ned warned them, "such evidence is not admissible in court."

Their faces fell.

"Then what good is it?" Moon asked.

"For information. If you know what's going on it's easier to fit the pieces together and to anticipate the next move. We may be able to catch them *doing* something. Anyway, I think it's worth a try."

"What luck did you have with the other juke box users?" Jean asked. "Did you get your resistance organized?"

Ned shook his head. "No luck at all. They're all going to take the new machines. They say the new models may stimulate business enough to make them pay off."

"That's a lot of baloney, isn't it?" Moon asked.

"I think so. I think the real reason is that they're scared," said Ned.

"Chickens!" Bruce said.

"I don't blame them too much," said Ned. "Most of them have children. They're afraid for them, and afraid for their businesses which mean their livelihood. I think the real blame lies with the ordinary citizens."

"What do you mean? How do you figure that?" Bruce asked.

"Well, people don't get as excited about lawbreakers as they used to. Lots of them break traffic laws and liquor laws themselves. They get used to closing their eyes to things. They don't want to get involved."

"But that's terrible!" said Jean indignantly.

"Yes, it is. And that's why gangsters get so bold. They have found that they can get away with it. And when they *are* brought into court, they know all the angles. That's why we don't want to go off half-cocked. We want to have some real evidence."

Bruce felt a slow anger building up inside him, and an impatience to start moving. "If we're going to plant that detectaphone, we had better get organized. We'll have to put it in before dark."

Ned looked at his watch. "It's almost six o'clock. You all go home and eat your dinner. You boys come back here about seven. I'll call Bill and find out about the machine. You'll have to install it, because I could never get upstairs to that loft."

"I helped put in an intercom once," Moon said. "I think I can figure this gadget."

They started down the street. Jean walked with Bruce. Honey and Moon came behind them.

"I have an idea," said Jean.

Bruce looked at her suspiciously. "If your idea is to help us tonight, you can forget it."

"What if the Mole comes along and catches you and Moon setting up that recorder? Then your plan will go kaput, and your little necks will go gurgle, gurgle!"

"And where do you come in?"

"Suppose there were someone strolling up and down the street. The Mole wouldn't dare go into the stable until the coast was clear. And if someone were to sing a certain song, you would know the Mole was coming and would have time to get out."

"The plan has some sense," Moon agreed.

Honey looked at Jean apprehensively. "This someone you are talking about—is it *one* someone, or is it *two* someones?"

"Now, Honey, wouldn't I look silly walking up and down the street singing all by myself?"

Honey nodded glumly. "That's what I was afraid of."

"I don't know about this," said Bruce. "The Mole isn't exactly crazy about any of us. He might catch you girls—"

"Out in the *street?* He wouldn't dare," said Jean. "Now what shall we have for our warning song?"

"How about, 'On Top of Old Smoky'?" Moon suggested. "You can make a lot of noise with that one."

"All right," Jean agreed, "and if you hear it, boys, you had better hurry."

They went their separate ways. Bruce fumed at the necessity of sitting through dinner with the family. When the meal was finally over, he ran all the way down to the Nook.

Moon was already there. Ned showed them the tiny German recorder. It was powered by four flashlight batteries. They put the instrument into an ordinary shoebox and tied it with string. The microphone cord plugged into the recorder through a small hole cut into the side of the box.

The boys planted the detectaphone before dark. A knothole near the floor in the upper room of the stable served perfectly to conceal it. They dropped the wire to the stall below and hid the shoebox behind a pile of furniture. Now all that remained to be done was to plug in the mike, but Ned had warned them not to do this until nine-thirty. They didn't want the tape to run out too soon.

They sat on the floor and waited for the time to pass. Soon they heard footsteps out on the sidewalk. Bruce ran to the window and peeked out cautiously. Then he relaxed as giggles floated back to them. The street light silhouetted two bouncing pony tails.

"It's only the palace guard," he said. "Maybe we should tell them we're all set up."

"And spoil their fun? They'd hate us," said Moon.

"Well, we'll let 'em go around the block a few times."

They waited a while, then plugged in the microphone and stepped outside. They stood there, both of them remembering Ned's last words to them. "When the machine's set, you're through. Go to bed and sleep. I'll come down in the morning and we'll see what's on the tape."

Bruce looked at Moon. "Do you want to go to bed?"

"Naw," said Moon.

"I think we ought to keep an eye on the girls until they quit marching and go home. Don't you?"

"It's our duty. It really is," said Moon piously.

Bruce raised his eyes to the old pine tree that spread its limbs beyond the stable. It was their old lookout tree. The cross pieces were still nailed to the trunk, forming a ladder for easy ascent.

"There's no better place to keep an eye out than up there," said Moon.

Bruce needed no encouragement. Getting the record was only half of it. He wanted to *see* what went on.

They climbed high enough to be hidden from the ground by the lower branches, then chose perches that gave them a view of the stable door and the sidewalk beyond the south fence.

There was a street lamp in the middle of the block. Each time their marching guard came within the circle of light, the boys could see their maneuvers. The girls hummed as they strolled, harmonizing an entire repertory of hit tunes. Once, as they entered the circle of light, there was a pause in their musical efforts. Moon let out a savage m-e-a-o-u-w, m-e-a-o-u-w.

Honey jumped, then grabbed Jean around the neck. Moon shook with laughter and nearly fell out of the tree. Bruce could see that Honey was trying to pull Jean in the direction of home. Jean held her ground, and Honey started off alone. But in a minute she came back and they resumed their walk.

"Boy, would they be furious if they knew we were safe up here in the tree." Moon chuckled. "I hope their feet hold out."

"It's kind of a dirty trick," said Bruce. "We should have told them we had finished."

The traffic thinned down on the boulevard and few cars passed on the side street. One by one, the lights went out in the houses. Blandford Hall was dark now except for the square of light that marked Hobart's window. Then that, too, faded, and Bruce heard the sound of the window being raised. The night light in the upstairs hall dimly outlined a figure at the window.

Bruce touched Moon and pointed. The man stood there looking out for some time. The boys were so intent on watching him that they forgot about the girls.

Then suddenly, loud and clear, came the song, "On top of old Smo—ky—all covered with snow!"

The Mole was coming!

10

A Tattletale Box and
a Broken Cup

Bruce tried to see the street through the thick pine branches.

"I lost my true lover—"

The girls voices were cut off. The only sound was the click of footsteps on cement. Whose footsteps? Bruce wondered, as his fingers gripped the rough bark of the pine until he felt the pain.

Beside him, Moon muttered, "Oh, where are those dumb girls?"

Bruce started down the tree. Even if he blew the whole show, he wasn't going to let the Mole get his hands on Jean.

Moon grabbed his collar and hung on. "Wait. I think they're coming."

The two girls appeared under the street light. They were not singing now, and they were walking very fast. They crossed the street. A moment later, the boys heard a door bang.

Bruce settled back on his limb, weak with relief.

Moon touched Bruce's arm. "Look," he whispered.

They saw a dark shadow move along the stable wall. The door swung open. Then closed. Bruce turned his attention to the back door of Blandford Hall. Hobart should be coming to the rendezvous before long. By tomorrow they might all know the answer to the mystery.

But Hobart did not come. The pine bough became more and more uncomfortable. Bruce wished that he were padded as well as Moon. They didn't dare move around for fear of attracting attention to the tree. Hobart was probably watching from his window. As the time dragged by, the boys began to regret their impulse to be eyewitnesses. The bells on Saint Pat's chimed eleven.

Now surely Hobart would come. Bruce felt hypnotized from staring into the dark. His eyeballs ached from watching the house. He didn't see the shadowy figure until it was almost under their tree. The man must have cut across the park from the east gate.

He paused just beneath the boys. If he looks up from this angle, Bruce realized, he can see us plainly.

Bruce's long legs dangled directly above the man's head.

The two boys held themselves rigid. The man looked toward Blandford Hall. Then he hurried to the stable, opened the door, and slipped inside.

"Whew," said Moon, letting out his breath. "That was close."

"Too close for comfort," Bruce agreed. "It was Foxy Frank, wasn't it?"

"Yeah." Moon changed his position. "I wish I'd brought a pillow."

"*You* should talk! My bones are sticking right through my skin.

It was probably thirty minutes later when the two men reappeared. They walked under the pine tree and crossed the park together.

The boys hurried to the stable and retrieved the detectaphone. Then they crossed to the house and Bruce unlocked the back door. Everything seemed quiet. They tiptoed up the back stairs to Bruce's room and undressed in the dark. It wasn't until they were in bed that they heard the footsteps overhead. Hobart was still searching the attic. He hadn't found what he had come for, and Bruce guessed that he was afraid to meet the Mole again empty-handed. But it was a bitter disappointment that he hadn't gone to the stable tonight. Bruce had planned on learning what Hobart was up to.

Moon was already breathing heavily. Bruce meant to stay awake until Hobart came out of the attic, but he was worn out from the vigil in the tree. Soon, he also slept.

The boys coaxed Cassie into giving them breakfast in the kitchen. Then Bruce called the girls while Moon got the shoebox from the bedroom. They met at the south gate.

"Hi," said Bruce. "Let's go."

Jean looked at him crossly. "Well, aren't you going to ask us about last night?"

"Yes," said Honey. "There we were—risking our lives—standing guard for you—"

Moon snickered.

Bruce said, "OK. Tell us about it."

"It sure took you guys long enough," said Honey. "We thought you must be *making* that detectaphone. We walked, and walked, and walked—"

"And all of a sudden," said Jean dramatically, "there was the Mole! We knew you were in there! We thought you would be trapped! Say, did you hear our warning song?"

"Yeah, we heard it," Bruce said.

"Well, you don't seem very impressed!"

"Oh, we are," said Bruce. "We're going to recommend both of you for the Congressional Medal of Honor!"

"With poison oak leaves," Moon added.

It was lucky that they reached the Nook just then. Bruce could see that the girls were mad.

Ned left the shade pulled down and locked the

door behind them. "Let's see what's on the tape," he said. "Maybe this will tie everything up."

"I'm afraid not," Bruce said. "Hobart didn't come. Just Foxy Frank."

Ned gave Bruce a sharp look. "How do you know that? You haven't heard the tape yet?"

Bruce knew he was trapped. "Me and my big mouth," he said.

"Moon, where were you two last night?" Ned demanded.

"In the pine tree," Moon admitted sheepishly.

"You *heels*," said Jean bitterly. "We might have known you wouldn't miss anything."

Honey looked at Moon suspiciously. "I'll bet you were that yowling tomcat."

"That was just an obbligato to that singing of yours. 'Meet me in Saint Louis—Louie,' " he warbled in a high falsetto.

"Oh, you let us walk and walk," said Jean furiously, "and you were up there all the time!"

"Well, this settles it," Ned told them sternly. "There will be no more roaming around in the night. Now let's run this tape."

The first sounds from the detectaphone were vague rustlings and scrapings. Then the Mole's voice growled, "About time you got here."

"What's eating you, Gito? I'm not late. The Englishman gone?"

"He never showed up. If he thinks he can snitch on the heist, he's got another think coming."

"Where does he fit in this picture?"

"He doesn't. Different set-up. I took him on as a favor to the bookies. Lord Hobart is in debt to the racing syndicate for fifty grand. If he doesn't come through, he's in trouble."

"What's his angle here?"

"That, Frankie, is none of your business. I'll deal with Hobart. You keep your mind on the juke box racket. You're in the big time now. Did you finish delivery?"

"All but one. No money there, anyway. A hole-in-the-wall place."

"All but one! Listen, you small-town jerk. One hold-out can blow the whole pay-off. Who is it?"

"A cripple down on the boulevard. Ned's Nook."

"A *cripple!* And two men couldn't handle him?"

"The boys knocked him around some, but he pulled a gun on them."

"So they ran? And by tomorrow every juke box joint in town will know about it. Frankie, get this through that blockhead of yours. We set up a town one hundred percent, and we furnish the muscle to back it up. We don't have hold-outs."

"So what do I do now?"

"Give him the works. And wind it up fast. This job is getting hot. And so is this place. We can't meet here much longer."

"Those kids still snooping around?"

"Yeah. And that jittery blue blood is giving me the willies. I'm not sure he's leveling about the loot.

Hobart had better deliver soon or he'll turn up missing."

The recorder picked up more noises. Then Frankie's voice said, "You going to wait for him, Gito?"

"No. We'll go down to your place and fix up a—"

That was all.

"Fix up a what?" Jean asked.

Ned looked grim. "I don't know. But I'm afraid it won't be long before we find out. One thing is clear—organized crime has come to town."

Bruce was bewildered. "But here—way out here in the Midwest? It couldn't happen here, could it, Ned?"

"It seems fantastic, but I'm afraid it's true."

"But this isn't New York or Chicago. We've never had gangsters here."

"They've found the juke box business is a good racket in the big cities. I suppose now they're after complete control."

"That makes me mad," said Bruce.

"Good!" Ned grinned. "Now, I think we should analyze what we have learned from this tape and decide what's to be done. First, the Mole's real name is Gito, and he is probably working for the head of the juke box racket. He hopes to feather his own nest with this little deal on the side. Second, Hobart has lost a large amount of money gambling on the horses, and there is something in Blandford Hall that he hopes to steal to pay this debt. And third, they are going to do something to the hold-out. That's me."

"Now do we have enough evidence to go to the police?" Honey asked.

"Actually, we still don't have too much to go on," said Ned. "Don't forget that this record can't be used in court. To get a guy like the Mole, you almost have to catch him in the act. These gangsters are slippery —and they're smart."

"But maybe he'll get you first," Jean pointed out.

Ned looked at Bruce. "The thing that bothers me is that we still don't know what Hobart is looking for. If the thing blows up now, Bruce may never solve that mystery."

"But you need protection, Ned," Bruce told him. "We all know that now."

Ned touched his black eye. "This is my combat star. I earned it and it made me feel good. I've been on the sidelines too long."

"But, Ned—"

"Now, just let me talk. This has always been a good, clean town—an old-fashioned town where kids can walk the streets in the evenings and folks don't need to lock their doors. Sure, we have our local bad boys like Foxy Frank—every town has them— but our police know them and keep them from bothering ordinary citizens. Now comes this thing, this strong-arm stuff, this organization stirring up our local thugs and muscling into legitimate business. Well, I'm not going to take it lying down."

"Hurray!" said Jean.

"I want more out of this deal than protection,"

Ned said. "I want to get the Mole and Foxy Frank. I want to break this racket wide open. But it's time you kids took cover. And I mean it! You stay off the streets and away from that stable!"

"Aw, Ned," said Moon.

"Bruce, will you tell your father I want to see him right after dinner tonight? I'll bring the recording. I'd like to have him hear it and get his advice on how to proceed."

"Why not now?" Bruce asked.

"I have some other things to do first. How about that drawing Mrs. Norton was going to make?"

"I forgot all about it," said Bruce. "It's in my dresser drawer."

"Will you get it? I have a friend at headquarters. I'll have him check the police files and see if he can identify Gito."

A customer rapped on the locked door. Ned glanced at his watch. "It's way past my opening time. Now you all go home and lay low today. And don't you kids *dare* to go outside your doors tonight. That's an order!"

Hobart did not look well at lunch. His color was more pasty and his hands shook more than usual. It made Bruce a little sick to look at Hobart. He had thrown away everything he should have treasured. He had completed the ruin his father had begun. Bruce was not proud of his father's cousin. He wished that Hobart had never come.

Bruce's mother interrupted his thoughts. "What time did you tell Mrs. Norton to come, Bruce?"

Bruce jumped. "Time? What for?"

"Bruce, this is *Friday*. It was *your* idea. Have you forgotten all about it?"

"Oh, yeah. It's Friday. I told her three o'clock— I think."

"And you invited the young people, too?"

"Yes, I did."

"Fine. Cassie is making crumpets. We'll use the Wedgwood china and the silver service. It is time you boys and girls learned a few of the amenities." Mrs. Blandford looked at her son, as she did sometimes, as though he were a little uncivilized.

Bruce felt like laughing. A tea party with the *amenities* was all that they needed to complete the madness of this crazy week.

Mrs. Blandford turned to her husband. "Will you be here for tea, Gregory?"

"Yes. I'm going to work on farm accounts this afternoon."

"Good. Will you join us, Hobart? Mrs. Norton is an artist friend of Bruce's. She is coming to see the Manet portrait."

Hobart dropped his cup. The fragile china shattered as the cup struck the saucer, and brown liquid splashed over the damask cloth. Hobart clutched at his throat and fell back in his chair, gasping for breath.

11

A Mad Tea Party

"Hobart!" cried Mrs. Blandford.

Gregory Blandford pushed back his chair. "I'll call a doctor."

Hobart opened his eyes and made an effort to control his labored breathing. "No—no—I'll be all right —as soon—as I get—my medicine."

Grandpa peered at him sternly. "Shouldn't smoke those black cigars—bad for the system."

"Grandpa, Hobart doesn't smoke cigars," said Mrs. Blandford.

"Does too. Smokes 'em before he goes to bed at night. I smell 'em."

Hobart put his hands on the table and pushed himself to his feet. "I say, I'm dreadfully sorry about the mess I made. If you don't mind, I shall remain in my room this afternoon."

"Sure you don't want a doctor?" Gregory asked.

Hobart shook his head, but he accepted his cousin's offer to help him upstairs. Bruce and Grandpa were left alone to eat their dessert.

"There's a bad one," Grandpa announced. "Don't know what he's doing here, but I'll wager he's up to no good."

"Why do you say that, Grandpa?"

"He prowls in the night." Grandpa gave Bruce a sharp look. "Matter of fact, so do you. What were you and Moon doing up in that tree?"

That's the way it was with Grandpa. Sometimes he was a million miles away. Then again, he could be as sharp as a tack.

"I'll tell you a secret, Grandpa. Moon and I are trying to solve a mystery. We're getting warm. You won't give us away, will you?"

"Nope. Funny thing—this Hobart puts me in mind of someone. Can't think who it is. Likely it will come to me one of these days."

Cassie came in with the dustpan. She scolded as she picked up the pieces of broken china. "I knew we shouldn't use the French china every day—it's thin as an eggshell. 'Tisn't as if Hobart was real company. Far as I know, nobody *invited* him. He acts like the Lord of the Manor, though, with Fergus running to his room every night with the electric percolator. Room service, that's what Hobart wants."

Bruce pushed back his chair. He must get the drawing down to Ned. But Fergus put his head in the door.

"Where have you been all forenoon, boy? There's chores waiting."

"All right. But I have to go down to Ned's for a minute first."

"Oh, no. You'll get down there jumpin' and hoppin'—"

"Twistin'," Cassie corrected.

"Same thing. You'll get down there and I won't see you till dinner."

"I promise I'll be right back." Bruce bolted before Fergus could reply.

It was amazing how much work Fergus could line up. Bruce had to hurry to get his chores finished before three o'clock.

Cassie had set out the silver service. Now she was frying crumpets on the griddle.

"Better make twice as many as usual," Bruce told her. "Moon is coming."

"Hollow legs? Dear me, I'll beat up another batch.

Now you carry the service to the front parlor. Then you go up and change your clothes. No blue jeans."

Cassie's getting bossier every day, Bruce thought. He was glad that he had cleaned up, though, when he and his mother greeted their four guests. The two girls wore fresh cotton dresses and teetered on high heels. Bruce had never seen Mrs. Norton in anything but a paint-spattered shirt and slacks. Today she looked pretty in a blue embroidered cotton, with her blond hair brushed into a soft bun at the nape of her neck.

Mrs. Norton raised her eyes to the stained glass window at the top of the stairs. "The window is so unusual and so very, very lovely."

"That is Bruce's great-grandmother," Mrs. Bland-ford said. "The family, however, thinks that it is a very poor likeness.

"Of course I wouldn't know about that," said Lucy, "but the colors in the glass are beautiful. It makes this hall seem like a little church."

"Father Blandford thinks a lot of the window, but it is the Manet portrait that really brings Lady Anne to life. I'll show it to you after we have had our tea."

They all went into the parlor where Cassie was waiting with hot buttered crumpets and strawberry jam. Moon tried hard to be polite. But Cassie winked at him and said, "Maybe you don't like my crumpets?" So Moon gave up the pretense and let his appetite run its normal course.

Mr. Blandford joined them. Bruce remembered that he had not yet made the appointment for Ned to see his father.

The conversation droned along politely. Outside the open windows lay the green park, empty and peaceful. Too quiet. Too peaceful. Bruce's skin prickled—his heartbeat thumped in his throat. Sometimes he had this feeling just before a thunderstorm —a feeling of apprehension. His eyes met Jean's, and somehow he knew that she felt it too. Time was running out. Something was bound to happen soon. And here they sat, drinking tea.

Finally his mother rose and asked, "Shall we start the gallery tour now? Gregory, why don't you come along and tell Mrs. Norton all about the Manet?"

They went upstairs and stood around the portrait. The late afternoon sun slanted through the stained glass window directly on the painting. Bruce had a feeling that there was something wrong—there was something queer about the Manet. He looked at Lucy Norton. She had a strange look on her face— a sort of embarrassment.

"My grandmother was on her honeymoon when this was painted," Gregory Blandford was explaining. "At that time Manet was a notorious, rather than a famous, painter."

Lucy stood there twisting her hands together, looking distressed. Bruce reached out and touched the canvas.

"Mrs. Norton, will you feel this?" he asked.

Lucy ran her sensitive fingers across the surface of the painting. Mr. Blandford looked at them questioningly.

"I don't understand," he said. "What's wrong?"

"The texture," Bruce told him. "You can *see* the blobs of paint, but you can't feel them."

Bruce's mother touched the painting. She turned a bewildered face to Mrs. Norton.

"I'm afraid this is not the original painting," said Lucy. "This is a color photograph, reproduced on a canvas textured paper."

"But that's impossible. The Manet can't be gone, it just can't be," Mrs. Blandford said. "Are you sure you're not mistaken?"

"She's right, Mother," said Bruce. "All you need to do is feel it."

"It seems odd that none of you noticed it," said Lucy.

"It has always hung there. We're so used to it we wouldn't think of examining it closely. I simply can't understand this."

"I can," said Moon. "The blue flash bulb."

Mrs. Blandford looked more bewildered than ever. "The blue what?"

Mr. Blandford had been looking at Bruce. "I'm sorry, son—about everything. I think it's time we had a talk, and this time I'll listen."

"We'll go now," said Lucy tactfully. "It was such

a lovely tea, and I'm so very, very sorry about the portrait."

She shooed her reluctant companions down the stairs and out through the side door.

Bruce glanced uneasily down the hall toward Hobart's room.

"Dad, let's go down to the library. We can talk better there."

Bruce and his parents went to the library and closed the door. Then Mr. Blandford said, "Now, Bruce, yesterday you told me the Manet was gone—"

"Yes, sir. When I came in from haying, that place on the wall was empty. I wish now that I had stayed right there. But I ran down to the stable to get you."

"And when we came back, the portrait—or, rather, the photograph—was hanging there. Do you have any idea who—"

"There was only one person in the house all yesterday afternoon—except Grandpa."

"Bruce, whom are you talking about?" asked Mrs. Blandford.

"Hobart."

"Bruce! Are you saying that Hobart stole the Manet?"

"Yes, I am. Or helped someone to do it. We found that blue flash bulb the night the Mole was in the attic."

"A *mole* in the *attic?*" Bruce's mother was completely confused now.

"Another thing," Bruce continued, "this noon, Hobart dropped his cup when you told him that Mrs. Norton was coming to see the Manet. How about that?"

Gregory's face was grim. "I think we have all been blind around here except you, Bruce. What else do you know?"

"Plenty. Some of it I tried to tell you, but you wouldn't believe me."

"I know. And I'm sorry. Now let's hear the whole story."

When Bruce had finished, his mother was crying.

"We've never felt that we could sell the Manet— and now it's gone. The money would have sent Bruce through college."

Bruce's father was furious. "My own cousin! Worming his way in here, letting us entertain him—then stealing the only thing of value that my father ever got from the estate! Come along. We're going to find out about this."

Hobart's door was locked. Gregory rattled the knob and knocked on the panel. "Hobart! Open the door. I want to talk to you."

There was a moan from inside. "I'm not well. I'm resting."

"Open this door!"

A moment of silence, then dragging footsteps. The lock clicked, and the door opened. Hobart tottered back to bed and pulled the blanket up to his eyes.

Gregory stood over him threateningly. "Hobart, where is it?"

"Where is what?"

"The Manet portrait."

"I don't know what you're talking about."

"Stop stalling. Is it here—in this room?"

"I know nothing about your portrait. Go away and let me alone. I'm sick."

"Yesterday, when you were here alone," said Gregory, "you took the real portrait and replaced it with a photograph. You changed them right here in your room, didn't you?"

"A fantastic story," said Hobart. "Who saw me do this?"

Bruce's heart sank. No one had actually seen him do it. No one could prove that he *had* done it.

Gregory did not give up easily. "Do you want to tell us where it is? Or shall we search your room?"

Hobart turned his face to the wall. "I refuse to discuss this matter any longer."

The search turned up nothing but racing forms, which Gregory tossed contemptuously upon the bed. "All right, cousin. We know about your racing operations, and we know about your debts. You're in a tough spot and you'd better do some fast thinking."

They left Hobart's room. Gregory lifted the fake Manet off the wall and carried it down to the library.

"What are we going to do now?" Bruce asked.

"I'm going to have this copy photographed, and then I'm going to send prints to art dealers and galleries. That way they can identify the portrait if it shows up."

"Oh, that reminds me, Dad. Ned wants to see you tonight."

"All right. Tell him to come on over."

Bruce wandered away. Suddenly he felt let down. Of course he was glad to have his father's confidence, but there were disadvantages. So far, he and Moon had done a pretty fair job of detection, but now they would have to step aside. Now the adults would be handling things. If we get a bunch of cops around, he thought morosely, they will blow the whole thing.

He was still puzzled about the theft of the portrait. It simply didn't fit in with Hobart's interest in the diary and his search of the house. They hadn't found the diary when they searched Hobart's room a little while ago. Bruce wondered what he had done with it.

On a sudden hunch he went to the attic and looked in the pocket of the Prince Albert coat. It was there! Hobart had replaced it. He sat down and carefully re-read all the passages concerning William and Basil, but he learned nothing that he hadn't known before. Then he heard the dinner gong. He went down to the dining room.

Grandpa came in fuming, "Who's taken Mother's portrait off the wall?"

"It's in the library," Gregory told him.

"What in tarnation is it doing in there?"

"Tack's loose," Gregory mumbled. "I'll put it back after awhile."

Fergus brought in the soup. "I took the tray up as you said, ma'am. Door's locked. He wouldn't answer."

"Too many cigars," said Grandpa.

Bruce was still thinking about the diary. "Grandpa, what did you bring from England when you came back that time?"

"Precious little. Basil saw to that."

"Just the portrait and the window?"

"Window? I didn't bring the window. Mother sent it when I built the house—had it made in the likeness of herself."

Well, that's that, thought Bruce. Hobart couldn't very well steal a window, and why would he want to, anyway?

It wasn't long after dinner that Ned's little car put-putted up to the side door. Bruce ran out, helped him with his crutches, and carried the detectaphone into the house.

"Did you identify Gito?" Bruce asked.

"I think so," Ned told him. "Of course, the sketch isn't like a photograph, but we feel practically certain that the Mole is Gito Partinelli, right-hand man of the Chicago juke box king."

"Golly," said Bruce. "A big-time gangster."

Mr. Blandford listened intently to the tape recording. When it was finished he said angrily, "There is more to this than catching a thief. This is something that affects the welfare of everyone in our town."

"I feel the same way," Ned agreed. "The time to

stop this kind of rot is before it gets started. Now that we know what we're up against, I don't think it's a job for the local police."

"F.B.I.?" Bruce asked.

"There is a new Special Group on Organized Crime," said his father. "They're experts in gathering evidence against these Fifth Amendment boys."

Ned nodded. "That's what I had in mind. They don't rush in until the time is ripe."

Bruce's heart thumped with excitement. This was big! They might have an undercover man right here in the house!

"The main thing," Ned continued, "is to see that Hobart doesn't run out on us before we can get set."

"I don't think he will," said Gregory. "Hobart is a very frightened man. I believe he's more afraid of the Mole than he is of us. According to this tape, he didn't go to the stable last night. He doesn't *dare* run until he has made the payoff."

"We want to catch Gito in our net," said Ned. "If we give him enough rope, maybe he'll try to get to Hobart—if Hobart doesn't come to him. In the meantime, we don't want these youngsters running around at night."

Gregory gave Bruce a stern look. "I'll see to that."

The two men made plans to meet in the morning and contact the proper authorities. Then Ned left.

Bruce got on the upstairs extension and started a telephone marathon. Bruce talked to Jean, who had already talked to Honey, who had talked to Moon.

Then Bruce talked to Moon, and they talked over what the girls had talked about. All this conversation came to one thing: they wished they had kept the mystery to themselves until they had solved it. Now they were all campused after dark, and it was a bore.

Bruce went down the hall and paused outside Hobart's closed door. He could hear him moving around inside. Bruce left his own door open. At least, he could stand guard. If Hobart left his room, Bruce was determined to follow him.

He undressed, got into bed, and turned out the light. He heard the chimes at eleven—eleven-thirty —twelve. It had been a long and exciting day. He felt limp and tired. His eyelids drooped and he fought off the drowsiness that stole over his body. He lay there —half asleep . . .

The blast raised him out of bed. The old house shook. Somewhere nearby a windowpane shattered and glass crashed to the ground below. His first thought was of an earthquake. He ran to the window. Lights were coming on in houses all around the park. Windows opened, voices called out.

A second blast shook the earth. Far away, a fire siren began to wail.

12

The Sky Came Tumbling Down

Bruce yanked on his clothes. He reached the front stairs along with his father, who wore his pajama top over his trousers. Grandpa, Cassie, and Fergus all appeared without their false teeth, and they looked like three old gnomes. Mrs. Blandford, in robe and curlers, was the last one out the door.

From every side of the park, people streamed toward Jackson Boulevard. Bruce thought of the old story, *Chicken Little*. "Hurry, hurry, the sky is tumbling down." He took off across the park at a dead run, pretending not to hear the voices calling to him.

As Bruce came through the west gate, Moon caught up with him. They ran on together toward the parked fire truck and the crowd of jabbering people that filled the street ahead. Squeezing, dodging, and pushing, they reached the front of the crowd.

In the place where Ned's Nook had been, there was now only a heap of bricks and splintered wood. The only thing in one piece was Ned's swivel chair; it sat like a throne upon the rubble. Again, Bruce felt the anger building up inside of him. Then Jean was there beside him and she was crying.

"Darn them!" she said. "Oh, darn them!"

"The works. They gave him the works."

They heard a stirring in the crowd. People were moving aside to make way for Ned's little car.

Ned surveyed the mess. "They play for keeps," he said ruefully. "Did any of you kids see anything?"

They shook their heads. "We were in bed—like you told us," Bruce reminded him.

"Anyone watching Hobart?"

Bruce's face flushed. "I was."

"This would be a good time for him to get to the Mole—or for the Mole to get to *him*."

Ned was right. Bruce knew that he had let him down, and he was ashamed. As he turned away and started for home, the police began pushing the crowd back to rope off the bombed area.

His father was pacing back and forth beside the house. He didn't reprimand Bruce for running off, but merely asked, "What was it?"

"Bomb. Blew up Ned's place."

"We'll go and tell Hobart."

The door was still locked and there was no response to their knock. Gregory pounded on the wood. "Hobart. Open the door this instant, or we'll force it open."

Finally, the lock clicked and Hobart let them in. He was pale and shaky and his bald head shone with drops of perspiration.

"Your little playmate has dropped a bomb," Gregory told him, "and I imagine he has another one waiting for you."

Hobart made no reply.

"If you give back the Manet portrait," Gregory continued, "I will not press charges against you. I will help you to get protection from these people— providing you tell us some things we need to know."

"You can't prove a thing," said Hobart.

"There are some things you yourself have proved," said Gregory angrily. "You've proved that you aren't fit to be a Blandford. You have violated our hospitality and brought danger to everyone in our family."

"I have nothing to say," Hobart insisted stubbornly.

"Very well. You can start packing. You leave here in the morning—alone. Perhaps your friend Gito will escort you to the airport."

The name *Gito* struck home. Hobart's eyes glazed with terror and his mouth trembled.

Gregory took the key out of the door and turned to Hobart. "There's no use going to the stable tonight. Gito isn't there. But just to prevent an impulsive departure, we'll lock you in."

Gregory turned the key in the lock.

"You aren't really going to let him go, are you?" Bruce whispered.

"A bit of a bluff," his father answered as he crossed the hall to Bruce's room. "Now I don't have to lock *you* in, do I?"

Bruce grinned at him sheepishly. "I guess not."

"All right. Good night, son."

Bruce was sure he wouldn't sleep a wink. His wrist watch read one o'clock. After he was in bed he tried to make a new plan for catching the Mole. But his thoughts kept getting fuzzy.

Bruce was awakened by the clatter of dishes and the smell of coffee. Out in the hall, Fergus set down a tray, unlocked Hobart's door, and carried the breakfast into the room. In a moment, he came out, locked the door, and crossed the hall to Bruce's room.

"How about bringing me breakfast in bed?" asked Bruce.

Fergus snorted. "His Royal Highness is the only one rates that service! I wouldn't be surprised if Cassie put poison in his coffee, she hates him that bad. Say, boy, what's this business about locking him in?"

"Protective custody," Bruce told him.

"There's a lot of hanky-panky going on around here that we don't know about," Fergus complained. "Things ain't been normal since he arrived."

"You can say that again!"

"Morning paper's full of the bombing. Wouldn't surprise me if Hobart had something to do with that, too. Now you get up. Cassie has enough to do without fixing late breakfasts."

Bruce needed no prodding. He was half dressed by the time Fergus had hobbled down the back stairs.

Gregory was talking on the telephone in the library. Bruce picked up the morning paper. Black headlines announced: PARALYTIC'S BUSINESS WIPED OUT BY UNKNOWN BOMBER. There was a picture of Ned in his wheelchair, taken last night beside the ruins. The story stated that there were no known witnesses to the bombing. The police had found no clues.

In a separate box, under Ned's picture, was a statement signed by himself. He told of being threatened by Frank Olachnavitch, and of being assaulted by two employees of the Triangle Music Company. He stated his theory that the bombing was the work of a syndicate which had moved into town for the purpose of wholesale extortion.

Jean, Honey, and Moon arrived before breakfast was over. Mr. Blandford beckoned to them to come into the dining room.

"A special federal agent is coming from Omaha today," he told them. "He is posing as a house guest. I hope I can depend on you youngsters to cease your detective activities now. The investigation will be in very capable hands. Above all, don't talk to anyone about what you know!"

Bruce wished that his father hadn't been so blunt. He could see that the others were offended at being pushed aside with no thanks for what they had done. Dad was worried that he and his friends would get hurt, Bruce knew, but he could have been more diplomatic.

Then Grandpa spoke up with his own theory about the bombing. "They were dynamiting down at the stone quarry last night. Henry Johnson would work day and night to make an extra dollar. He drove a hard bargain, too, when I built this house."

Moon's glum face broke into a grin. Jean and Honey giggled. They all knew that Henry Johnson had been dead for fifty years and the stone quarry buildings were crumbling ruins.

Cassie gave Grandpa an affectionate look as she filled his coffee cup and handed him another hot popover. "Here, Mr. William, have another one before I turn these kids loose."

Cassie's popovers were tender and crisp. The four friends filled them with strawberry jam and took them along in paper napkins. They headed for Jackson Boulevard.

Their hunch that Ned would be at the ruins proved to be correct. He was sitting in his car, watching two policemen poke around in the debris.

"Ned, did you have any insurance?" Bruce asked.

Ned shook his head. "The premium was too high. Figured my little stock wasn't worth it. I didn't plan on getting blown up with a bomb, though."

"Aren't you scared?" Honey asked. "They may try to get *you* next time."

Ned laughed. "That bomb may hurt them more than it does me."

"How do you mean?" Moon asked.

"My home phone has been ringing all morning. Five guys have changed their minds. Now they're willing to testify that Olachnavitch put the squeeze on them."

"But what about Gito?" Bruce asked. "He's really behind this."

Ned shot a warning glance at Bruce, and jerked his head in the direction of the policemen. "Sh-h-h. We're keeping that angle quiet. We'll make a special rope for him."

Bruce looked at the mess of rubble. "Isn't there something we can do?"

Ned shook his head. "The police don't want anyone else poking around here."

"But we feel so helpless," Jean complained.

"There is something you can all do," Ned told them. "Get your parents to write to the newspaper, and to the mayor, and the county attorney. This is a good time to stir people up. We want to make this town too hot for gangsters. Tell them about the juke box racket—but not a word about the Mole. Understand?"

Jean brightened. "We'll do it. We'll get the neighbors to write, too."

"Fine. But stay away from Blandford Hall. We want everything quiet around there."

13

Protective Custody

When Bruce reached home, he went upstairs to his room. The key was still on the outside of Hobart's door, and Bruce could hear him moving around inside.

Bruce stretched out on his bed with his eyes on the door across the hall. No one came near. Watching Hobart was getting pretty boring. He hadn't left that room for twenty-four hours. What was he doing? What was he thinking?

At noon, Bruce went down to the kitchen.

"Has Hobart had any lunch?" he asked Cassie.

"No, and it would do him good to go without," she snapped.

Bruce walked up behind her and tugged at a stray wisp of hair on her neck. "Aw, Cassie, please fix something and let me take it up. I'm detecting. Don't you want to help me?"

Cassie slapped at his hand. "Let me be, young pup."

Bruce pushed his face close to hers. "I *must* get into that room. He's hiding something there! It might be a-a-ugh!" He staggered, clutched at his chest, and pretended to faint.

"Oh, stop your tomfoolery. I'll fix his lunch, but he'll get it on the kitchen crockery, the clumsy ox."

Bruce followed her around the kitchen, sampling the luncheon dishes.

"Keep your fingers out of things," said Cassie. Then she added, "What do you think Hobart is up to?"

"Oh, so you are curious. You do want to know," Bruce teased. "Give me that tray and I'll find out."

Bruce unlocked the door and opened it. Hobart was still in pajamas, and looked as though he hadn't slept much. His wig was crooked on his round head, and there was a gray look around his mouth. A chair had been pushed close to the window as though he had been sitting there looking out. Most of his breakfast was still on the tray.

"I brought your lunch." Bruce put the tray table down and pulled up a chair beside it. "Sit down and eat. I'll wait and take both trays back with me."

"No need."

"I'll wait," Bruce repeated.

Hobart sat down and picked up the cup of steaming coffee. Even when he used both hands, it slopped over.

"Taking the Manet was a pretty lousy thing to do," Bruce said.

"Why do you keep talking about that?"

"I guess because I know you stole it. I can't figure out how you could do a thing like that, with all those blue-blooded Blandfords behind you. How could you turn into such a mess? How could you sink so low?"

Hobart looked up angrily. "You can't talk to me like that!"

"Why not? You haven't done one thing to earn our respect. Hobart, why don't you tell the whole story?"

"What story?"

Hobart's stubbornness infuriated Bruce. "Oh, come on! We're not all dopes around here. I know you met Gito in the stable, because I was there. I found the diary in your coat pocket. I've seen you searching the house, and switching the pictures. Now you have the Manet, but it isn't going to help you, is it? Because that portrait is hot. Every art dealer in the country is watching for it to turn up. Even Gito can't get rid of it—not now. So you're in trouble. You have to deliver something else. What, Hobart? What are you looking for?"

Bruce knew that he had guessed the truth, for Hobart turned livid with rage.

"Get out of here! Get out!"

"All right. But if I were in your shoes, I'd choose the law before I took my chances with Gito. He isn't going to let you get away—you can be sure of that. When you leave today, he'll be waiting for you somewhere out there."

Bruce picked up the breakfast tray and left the room. He locked the door again and went downstairs to lunch. His father was the only one at the table.

"Mr. Thornton is arriving on the afternoon plane," he told Bruce. "We are pretending that he is an old friend."

"Is Hobart leaving?" Bruce asked.

"Hobart isn't going anywhere. Hobart is our decoy. Now you remember instructions. Stay in the house, and don't do anything!"

Whose case is this, anyway, Bruce thought resentfully. *We* did the investigating. We got it all set up for them. And now we're supposed to run along and stay out of the way. He didn't say anything, though. He went back to his room.

The afternoon wore on. On the surface, everything seemed normal. Somewhere in the front of the house, Fergus vacuumed the rugs. Mrs. Blandford and Cassie sewed in the downstairs sitting room. Hobart paced back and forth behind the locked door of his room.

Bruce tried to concentrate on an historical novel. Last week it had seemed very exciting, but today he found himself reading the same paragraph over and over again.

Today was Saturday. He thought about last Saturday night, and it seemed a long, long time ago. There had been a gang of junior high school kids down at Ned's. They danced to the juke box, drank soda, and Indian wrestled—just horsed around and had fun. Then he walked home with Jean, and they sat in the porch swing and talked for a long time. He saw Jean almost every day, but they never ran out of something to talk about. Sometimes they argued, and sometimes they quarreled, but they always had plenty to discuss.

He had taken other girls to school events a few times, but somehow he felt uneasy with them. He never knew what to say. With Jean it was different. She never tried to be smart or sophisticated. She was always herself, and he didn't have to try to figure out what she meant when she said something.

That wasn't all, though. He liked her brown eyes under straight brows, and the smooth way she wore her hair. He liked her laugh that rang out like a song. He had read somewhere that people seldom married a childhood friend. He thought about the long years of school ahead—three years of senior high—then college. He supposed that Jean would start dating someone else before long. He knew that it would hurt him when she did. But why should she wait around for him? He wasn't especially good at anything. He wasn't a wheel at school—and he didn't know what he wanted to do when he finished his schooling.

Tonight he wouldn't see Jean. Now there wasn't any Ned's Nook. A week ago he hadn't even heard of Cousin Hobart or Foxy Frank or the Mole. Thinking about it now, it seemed like a nightmare. Bruce felt as though he would explode. Why didn't something happen? How long was Hobart going to stay in that room?

Mr. Thornton arrived just before dinner, and the family went into the dining room—all except Hobart. Gregory had unlocked the bedroom door and told Hobart to come down to dinner, but he had received no reply.

To Bruce's disappointment, Mr. Thornton didn't mention his work. He seemed in no hurry to start investigating anything. Instead, he got Grandpa talking about the old days on Moreton's Pup Farm. Bruce heard, for the hundredth time, about the Grand International Scurry Cup race when Lord Falmouth had shipped his twenty-five thousand dollar thoroughbred racer out to Iowa. Then, Grandpa told how he and two of Lord Ducie's sons had strung up the first telephone in the county between the House of Lords' Tavern and Moreton's farm. "So he could keep tab on his Pups," Grandpa explained.

Fergus always liked to put in his oar when the talk turned to the old days. "Tell about the hayrack racing," he urged.

So the talk went on and Bruce became more and more restless. Grandpa had a way of adding flourishes, digging up new bits of color from the garden of memory. The coffee cups were refilled and emptied again, and still they sat at the table.

"Yes, there were high-jinks in those days," Grandpa said. "I recall the night Lord Vincent's youngest son —Archie, it was—rode right into the House of Lords' Tavern on his thoroughbred mare. He picked up the barmaid with one arm and rode off with her."

Bruce's laughed died in his throat as he looked up and saw Hobart standing in the doorway. He was dressed with meticulous care. All his bravado was gone. His face looked crumpled, as though the flesh had receded from beneath the skin. His shoulders sagged.

The room was suddenly very still. Everyone looked at Hobart.

"I'm done for," he said in a tired voice, "and I might as well admit it."

14

Hobart's Last Race

Bruce could scarcely contain his excitement. At last Hobart was going to talk!

"Sit down, Hobart," said Gregory.

Fergus filled Hobart's coffee cup; then he started fussing around with the dishes.

"You can do that later," Gregory told him. Fergus took the hint and left the room. But Bruce could see Cassie's gray head behind the window in the butler's pantry. Her hearing was fine for an old woman. Bruce knew they both would be eavesdropping there.

Hobart glanced questioningly toward Mr. Thornton. Gregory introduced the agent and explained his presence in the house.

"Before you say anything," the investigator told Hobart, "I would suggest that you call a lawyer."

Hobart shook his head. "No. It would serve no purpose. I'm ready to talk now, and I want to get it over with."

Grandpa had been staring at Hobart ever since he had entered the room. Suddenly he said, "Edith. I knew all the time he reminded me of someone—Edith."

No one answered him. They all looked at Hobart. Bruce thought it was a bit like the moment before the curtain goes up on a play. Then Hobart began to talk. It was a sordid story and a rather sad one. Hobart had spent his childhood holidays trailing after his parents from one race track to another. He was sent down from Oxford for bookmaking among the students. He had never held a job in his life. He lived by gambling. Sometimes he was flush, sometimes penniless, but he always had connections which enabled him to borrow money until he won again. That was the story of his life: England, Ireland, Scotland, and Europe, then the West Indies. About a year ago he had come to the United States, still following the races. He hit a long losing streak, and at last there was no one who would give him a stake. He borrowed from a gambling syndicate. His luck went from bad to worse. Now he owed fifty thousand dollars and the syndicate meant to collect it—one way or another.

"And Basil had told you that the portrait was valuable?" Gregory asked.

"No. I didn't even realize the portrait was a Manet until Bruce told me. I didn't want the portrait, you see."

Bruce was confused. "But you did take it."

"Yes, I took it. But only because I didn't find what I came for. And Gito was pushing me. We decided to photograph the portrait. He thought he could get it sold before you discovered the substitution."

"Then Gito has the painting?" Gregory asked.

Hobart shook his head. "He gave me the photograph. I was to put it in the frame and bring the original to the stable that night. But I—I didn't go."

"Then where is the original?"

"In the attic, fastened with adhesive tape to the under side of the billiard table."

Bruce breathed a sigh of relief. At least, the Manet was safe.

"But what *did* you come for?" Gregory asked.

"Grandmother's emeralds."

Everyone looked blank.

"That is why I wanted to read the diary," Hobart continued. "But there was nothing in it that I didn't already know. There was nothing more about the emeralds."

Grandpa banged the table with his fist. "He accused me of stealing them, he did."

"Who did?" Gregory asked.

"Basil. My black-hearted brother."

Gregory was puzzled. "When, Father? I thought you never heard from Basil after you left England."

"A letter came after Mother's funeral. He wanted to know what I'd done with the emeralds. I never saw them after that night when we had the quarrel."

Gregory turned to Hobart. "I don't understand. What made you believe that the emeralds were here?"

"My father had been after Lady Anne to insure the emeralds, or put them in the bank for safekeeping. You see, they were the choicest gems from the Colombia mine. They were extremely valuable. After she broke the necklace that night, there was a great to-do until they'd all been found. Basil offered to take them to the bank—"

Grandpa snorted derisively.

"—but my grandmother, Lady Anne, said she would do it herself. She never wore the emeralds again, and when Basil asked her about them, she told him that she had taken care of the matter. She said the jewels were safe. When they opened the bank vault after her death, the emeralds were not there. My father said they searched Old Blandford Hall from attic to cellar. The jewels have never been found."

Grandpa shook with laughter. "So Basil was done out of them, after all."

"Father was always sure they were here somewhere," Hobart continued, "so I thought I'd have a go at searching for them."

Thornton broke the silence that followed. Turning

to Gregory he asked, "Do you want to press charges against your cousin?"

Gregory shook his head. "No. I only want to be rid of him."

Hobart turned pale. "If I leave, they'll kill me!"

"Indeed, I couldn't care less," Gregory said coldly.

"Our main objective now," said Thorton, "is to get Gito Partinelli. We've been after him for years. If we give you protection, Hobart, will you be willing to help us?"

Hobart rubbed a shaking hand across his face. Then he straightened his shoulders and said, "Yes. Yes, I will."

"Good. Now let's see what we have to work on. We can't get Gito on the juke box jacket because Foxy Frank will never squeal on him. We have breaking and entering—Bruce and Moon saw him in the attic. We have assault and battery—Bruce again. We can't charge conspiracy to commit a felony unless we involve Hobart."

"It sounds thin," said Gregory.

"But we have some trumps," said Thornton. "Gito doesn't know we have connected him with Olachnavitch. He doesn't know we have found out about the painting, and he doesn't know that Hobart has confessed. He *does* know that the town is stirred up over the bombing. He knows that his time is running out. What does he think about now?

"Gito is greedy," Thornton continued. "He thinks about getting his share of the loot from Hobart before it's too late. And Gito has a boss too—the big boss. He can't go back to him empty-handed. So he worries about Hobart running out on him. He is watching Hobart. He must make contact."

Hobart watched Thornton, listening intently to every word he said. Then his eyes turned to Gregory, and he seemed to flinch from the contempt in his cousin's face. He began to shake and his breathing turned into the heavy rasping that prefaced his attacks. He pushed back his chair. "My medicine—"

"Bruce, run and get it for him," said Mrs. Blandford.

"No. Please. I must lie down—I must rest. I'll be there—if you want me."

Gregory started to follow Hobart.

"Let him go," Thornton said calmly.

Bruce felt sorry for his mother. She looked terribly upset. "Aren't we going to do something?" she asked, of no one in particular.

Thornton poured himself another cup of coffee from the pot. Then he just sat there, drinking. Bruce folded his napkin and shuffled his feet. He leaned, first on one elbow, then on the other. How could they sit there, doing nothing? He picked up a spoon and balanced it on his forefinger. It swayed back and forth like a teeter-totter. Then it clattered to the table.

His father looked at him with annoyance. "I think you may be excused now," he said.

"Thanks," said Bruce, as he fled from the room.

He ran up the front stairs to the third floor. He was worrying about the Manet in the attic. Just to be sure Hobart didn't have a change of heart, he had better move the portrait to a safe place. He crawled under the billiard table and looked up. The canvas was taped flat to the under side. Bruce ripped it loose, and, without glancing at the canvas, he rolled it up. Then he wriggled out from under the table.

Now where shall I put it, he wondered. He walked over to the window and looked out. The afterglow had faded from the sunset and the park lay in twilight, not yet dark, but dimming fast.

Bruce heard a door close. In a moment, Hobart appeared on the lawn below. He wore his straw hat. In one hand he carried his light, overnight bag; in the other, a long, rolled-up parcel, the same length as the one Bruce held in his hand. Hobart moved a little way toward the stable, then stopped and looked behind him. He seemed to hesitate. Then he turned and walked quickly away from the stable, across the park toward the north gate.

For a moment Bruce felt numb, uncomprehending. Then he was hot with anger. Hobart had tricked them! He had planted a fake up here! And he was running out with the real Manet!

Bruce flung the canvas from him and raced for the back stairs, leaping down them three at a time. He jumped off the back porch at a run and sprinted after Hobart.

Hobart turned and cried hoarsely, "Go back!" Then he swerved to the right and started running toward the Maze.

The sound of the shot brought Bruce's head around. The Mole was cutting across the lawn from the stable. He was shooting at Hobart as he ran.

Bruce's mind ceased to function, but his legs carried him on toward the Maze. He was coming in at an angle between Hobart and the Mole. Hobart was staggering now and weaving from side to side.

Bruce looked back. The Mole was bearing down upon him. His arm was raised; the gun was pointed.

"Get out of the way," Gito screamed.

Bruce ducked and a bullet whined over his head.

Hobart was staggering badly as he reached the Maze. He disappeared between the high sides of the boxwood hedge.

Bruce zig-zagged on. Another bullet whined and pierced the boxwood. He stretched his legs for the last few yards. Then he was within the Maze.

15

The Mole in the Maze

Bruce almost stumbled over Hobart, who had dropped to his hands and knees. He was breathing in wheezing gasps, and he moved his head from side to side like a sick animal. Bruce snatched up the brown paper-wrapped roll and pulled Hobart to his feet.

"Lean on me—but *walk*—hurry."

He half dragged Hobart to the first turn. As they entered the second lane he heard the Mole behind them. Bruce knew their lives depended on his making the right turns—and the Mole making the wrong ones.

Hobart seemed dazed, and he leaned more and more heavily against Bruce. They made another turn —then Hobart went limp and slumped to the ground. He had lost consciousness.

On the other side of the boxwood, the Mole walked stealthily, seeking for the turn that would bring him to his victims. It would be only a matter of time until he blundered into this lane. Bruce knew he must move—he was only one turn ahead of the Mole.

To free his hands, he pushed the Manet inside the back of his shirt. Then he turned Hobart onto his back and grasped him under the armpits. It took all of his strength to drag the man's dead weight. Somehow, he made the next turn.

Beyond the Maze he heard voices, a few at first, then more and they seemed to be coming from every direction.

"Bruce!" It was his father's voice. "Bruce, are you in there?"

He opened his mouth to reply, then closed it quickly. He dared not answer. His voice would betray their position to the Mole. He tugged at his burden, inching his way along, making a left turn, then a right, trying to concentrate upon the familiar pattern of the Maze. He must not become confused. A mistake now would be fatal.

Once he heard the Mole breathing just over the wall of boxwood. Bruce stood very still until the sound receded. Then he moved again, dragging Hobart's dead weight. One more turn—then another—

a lane—another turn—the last lane—then the center of the Maze.

He dragged Hobart to one side of the grassy square. It was dark now. Bruce could see the blur of Hobart's white face, but he could not tell whether he was alive or dead. Bruce was winded. He stretched out on the grass for a moment, trying to catch his breath. He listened to the babble of voices outside the Maze. He could imagine their dilemma. They must have heard the shots, so they knew that Gito was armed. If they went in after him, Gito would have the advantage. If Gito came out, they assumed that he would be using Hobart or Bruce as a shield.

Thornton's voice called out, "Gito, toss your gun over the top and come out with your hands up!"

Fat chance of his doing that, Bruce thought. Whatever is done must be done inside. And there's nobody here but me.

Bruce stood up. He was scared, but he knew what he was going to do. Walking on cat's feet, he entered the dim green corridor. In the dark, this would be like playing a grim game of blind man's bluff. At the first turn, he dropped to his hands and knees and looked cautiously out into the next lane. Then he sprinted to the next turn, and once again dropped to the ground. At the third turn, he heard footsteps. He crouched low and waited.

There was only a whisper on the grass, like the slithering of a snake, then a pair of legs at Bruce's eye level. Bruce let him make the turn, then he tackled him around the knees. The Mole went down on his face, and the gun in his hand discharged. Before the man could move, Bruce let go of his legs and stepped on his arm, wresting the gun from his fingers. He gave the gun a mighty heave over the top of the boxwood.

"Come in and get him!" he yelled.

Then the Mole was on his feet. His hands were on Bruce's throat, and Bruce was fighting for his life. He beat with his hands upon Gito's powerful arms and kicked at his shins. He fought for air as the fingers dug relentlessly into his aching throat.

Then Moon's round face appeared at Gito's shoulder.

"Heavy, heavy hangs over thy head," he crooned as he hit Gito with a heavy object. Gito staggered, dropped his hands from Bruce's neck, and turned with a snarl to attack Moon. Then Thornton was there with a gun pushed against Gito's back.

The hall clock chimed ten as Bruce and his friends went into the dining room. Only two hours ago, Bruce thought, we were sitting here listening to Hobart's confession. It's been quite a rumble since then!

Gito Partinelli, alias the Mole, was in jail, charged with assault with intent to kill. If convicted, he faced a sentence of up to thirty years. Hobart, accompanied by the Blandfords, had been taken to the hospital in an ambulance. The brown parcel Hobart had carried proved to be nothing but wrapping paper. He had told the truth when he said the real Manet was in the attic.

The police had left, and the neighbors had gone home. Grandpa was in bed and asleep. At his age, mystery and violence left him undisturbed.

But Ned was there, looking very happy for a man who had lost most of his possessions.

"It will be a cinch now to convict Foxy Frank of extortion," he said. "Since the bombing, everyone's jumping on the bandwagon. There'll be no juke box racket in this town."

Cassie brought in a pitcher of lemonade and a plate of steaming cinnamon bread which she offered first to Bruce.

"Here," she said gruffly, "take a couple of pieces before it gets around to you-know-who."

Honey giggled and looked at Moon. Jean had eyes only for Bruce. Her face glowed as she said, "I died a thousand deaths when you were in the Maze. I mean, I simply died."

"And you captured him single-handed," Honey added.

Bruce felt his sore neck. "Not exactly single-handed. If Moon hadn't conked him when he did, I might not be here to tell about it."

"If you hadn't been looking out the attic window, Hobart would be dead and the Mole gone with the wind," said Ned. "Bruce, how do you figure Hobart's action?"

"We had just been talking about decoying Gito into some violent action—something they could charge him with. I think Hobart deliberately drew him out by pretending to run away with the Manet."

Mr. and Mrs. Blandford joined them.

"It was a heart attack," Gregory told them. "Hobart is in serious condition. The doctor says he doesn't understand how Hobart has lived this long. He has an organic heart condition, aggravated by years of hard living. The exertion and excitement tonight were too much."

Mrs. Blandford looked worried and bewildered. "So much has happened, and I don't understand half of it. It's a wonder I didn't have a heart attack myself when Bruce was in the Maze with that awful man!"

Gregory patted her shoulder. "Sit down and have some lemonade, dear. Everything is cleared up now."

"Not everything," said Bruce.

His father looked at him questioningly.

"Lady Anne's emeralds," Bruce told him.

Bruce's four friends looked at him in astonishment.

"Forget that wild story," Gregory told him. "There isn't a scrap of evidence that the emeralds were ever here. Don't you think my father would have found them?"

"I guess so. But I keep thinking about them. Something keeps nibbling at the back of my brain."

"What about the emeralds?" Jean asked. "Have we missed out on something?"

"That's what Hobart was looking for," Bruce answered. "He told us the emeralds have never been seen since the night of the quarrel."

Jean's eyes grew big with excitement. "Oh, Mr. Blandford, don't you have a desk with secret drawers, or an old tin box, or something like that?"

Gregory laughed. "Don't forget that Father built this house two years after he left England. And he brought nothing with him from England except the Manet portrait. No, I'm afraid you'd better forget about the emeralds."

Bruce had been staring into space with a glazed look in his eyes. "The day of the play—the day we picked up the beads—there was something odd about the carpet."

"Yeah," Moon agreed. "I kept trying to pick up little pieces of green light."

Bruce jumped to his feet. "That's it! Oh, what dopes we've been!"

He raced out of the room, and the others followed him. He switched on the lights in the front hall, and pointed to the stained glass window over the stairway.

"Look! Lady Anne is *wearing* them!"

A tiara of green stones crowned the lady's high-swept auburn hair, and three strands of the stones encircled her neck.

"The window is made of glass," Gregory objected.

"But the *jewels* could be real," Bruce insisted. "Lady Anne sent Grandpa the window. She had it made especially for him. She could have had the real emeralds set into the stained glass."

Gregory gazed at the window, and the disbelief on his face changed to conviction. "By George, I think you're right. The jewelry does have a different appearance from the glass in the rest of the window. The pieces are much smaller, and you can see the facets of the cut."

Bruce stared at the window as though he had never seen it before. "For seventy years Lady Anne has been looking down from that window, begging you to see the gift she gave to Grandpa. But no one ever noticed."

"The window was there before I was born," said his father. "You don't think about the things you see every day. Tomorrow we'll dig one of the jewels out of the lead and take it to an expert. If these prove to be the emeralds, you can go to any college you choose, Bruce."

16

A Toast to Sahara

Bruce and Moon gazed proudly at the new sign they had just nailed to the front of the old furniture store on Jackson Boulevard. The sign was hand painted and colorful. Lucy Norton had sketched a comical camel ridden by two perky teen-agers, and Jean and Honey had painted it. The foot-high letters spelled out the name.

SAHARA CLUB
Dry as the Desert
Manager: Ned Neeley

The club had been Grandpa's idea. After the emeralds were pronounced genuine (and the valuation far exceeded everyone's dreams), Grandpa had said to Bruce, "You found 'em. I'm going to do something for you—and for the town. I don't need this money myself, and I don't hanker for a fancy tombstone—rather see folks enjoy themselves. Now what about this young friend of yours in the wheelchair?"

So the month since the Mole's capture had been a busy one. The club was to be a recreation center. It was organized with a student board of directors. Ned would be supervisor and manager. Grandpa bought the building. The high school boys and girls and their parents supplied the labor.

Ned's shop was in the front of the building and he would operate it for his own profit. It was his idea to use the plate-glass show windows for displaying hobby projects of high school students.

Dividers set off the middle room for games. There was a shuffle board, dart boards on the walls, and the Blandfords' billiard table.

The large dance floor at the back of the building was ringed with tables and chairs like a real night club. Grandpa had bought a new juke box outright, and the *take* from it would go into the club treasury. Lucy Norton had a delirious time decorating the walls. Palm trees stretched to the ceiling, veiled women drew water from wells, and camels marched toward a distant oasis. Half a dozen girls had painted under her direction.

Now the club was finished and ready for the opening tonight. The five of them were left alone for the first time since the project was begun. Bruce suddenly realized that he hadn't seen much of Jean lately. He looked at her. She had been using a paint roller and her face was covered with fine, green freckles. He laughed.

"You look like a freak," he said.

"Thank you for noticing," she retorted crossly.

"Well! What's wrong with you? What have I done?"

"Nothing you would understand, you zombie. You've been off there somewhere in the twilight zone."

"We just haven't seen you except down here," said Honey.

"The answer is pretty gruesome," Moon told them. "He's been buried in the public library."

"During vacation?" Honey asked incredulously. "What a waste of time."

Jean gave Bruce an odd look, but he could see that she was no longer mad. Ned took five sodas out of the cooler and opened them.

"Let's drink a toast to Sahara," he said. "May it always be an oasis of happiness."

Honey looked around the room. "It still seems like a dream."

"A big, clean dream," said Ned, "for a big, clean town."

"I wish Hobart could have seen this," said Bruce.

"After all, if he hadn't come, we never would have found the emeralds."

They were all silent, thinking of Hobart, who had died two days after the Mole was captured.

"He made an awful mess of his life," said Bruce.

"But he did all right with his curtain scene," Jean answered.

"I'm glad Dad sent his body home to England. I think what he did that last night earned him the right to be buried in the cemetery at Old Blandford Hall."

"Why don't you tell them what you've been doing at the library, Bruce?" Ned suggested. "It all grew out of this thing."

"Well, I've been reading books on organized crime."

"But why?" Jean asked.

Bruce answered slowly, feeling for words that would express his ideas. "I've been doing a lot of thinking— about everything. About how Grandpa came here when this part of the country was newly settled. He had to fight cattle rustlers and claim jumpers, grass-hoppers and drought. He worked hard and he helped to build this town. There was a lot of excitement in those days."

"Yeah," said Moon. "And what have we got now? Nothing!"

"That's what I thought. I thought there was nothing left for us to do. Then I found out about Gito and Frankie and their kind. I guess you have to fight them just the way people had to fight the outlaws and con men in the old days. I guess we have to fight to keep what our grandfathers won for us. I guess every generation has its own challenge."

Ned nodded. "A guy doesn't talk a lot about love of country or about liberty under law and freedom of individual choice. You just don't wave that kind of thing around. But that is really what this is all about. The right to have, or not to have, a juke box may seem like a small thing, but to be pushed around by men like Foxy Frank and Gito is a large thing. If gangsters ever get bigger than the law, we'll be living in a jungle."

"I see what you mean," Bruce said. "This juke box thing is sort of basic, really, to the kind of country we want to live in."

Jean was looking only at Bruce when she said, "So what are you going to do about it?"

"I'm going to college and study political science. And then I'm going to law school. Mr. Thornton says that's the kind of training I need for what I want to do."

Jean's eyes were big and shiny as she said, "I think that's wonderful!"

Suddenly it seemed that the two of them were alone in the room. As Bruce looked at Jean, all the things he had been worrying about began to shrink and fade away. He needn't feel like such a worm! Now he knew where he was headed. And there was no reason why he and Jean couldn't keep right on going together. Next year he could drive a car. Then he could compete on equal terms with all the guys.

In the meantime, there was tonight. He wasn't thinking so much of the dance. He was thinking of the walk home afterwards, with Jean's hand in his.